A Candlelight Ecstasy Romance™

HIS SMILE LEFT HER BREATHLESS EVEN BEFORE HE BEGAN TO KISS HER AGAIN. . . .

This time the pressure of his mouth alternated between gentle insistence and hard demand until she responded, wildly returning his kisses.

Awash with sensation, she sat on his lap with her head nestled against his shoulder. She hadn't the will to move and couldn't even manage to open her eyes when he abandoned his exploration of her mouth and trailed his lips across her cheek to her temple.

"Did Gordon ever make you feel this way?"

"I'm not sure," she murmured dreamily. A mischievous sparkle danced in her half-open eyes. "Maybe if you kissed me again, it would help me decide."

WILD AND TENDER MAGIC

Rose Marie Ferris

A CANDLELIGHT ECSTASY ROMANCE™

Published by
Dell Publishing Co., Inc.
1 Dag Hammarskjold Plaza
New York, New York 10017

Dell ® TM 681510, Dell Publishing Co., Inc.

Candlelight Ecstasy Romance™ is a trademark of
Dell Publishing Co., Inc., New York, New York.

ISBN: 0–440–19411–3

Printed in the United States of America
First printing—October 1982

To Our Readers:

We have been delighted with your enthusiastic response to Candlelight Ecstasy Romances™, and we thank you for the interest you have shown in this exciting series.

In the upcoming months we will continue to present the distinctive sensuous love stories you have come to expect only from Ecstasy. We look forward to bringing you many more books from your favorite authors and also the very finest work from new authors of contemporary romantic fiction.

As always, we are striving to present the unique, absorbing love stories that you enjoy most—books that are more than ordinary romance.

Your suggestions and comments are always welcome. Please write to us at the address below.

Sincerely,

The Editors
Candlelight Romances
1 Dag Hammarskjold Plaza
New York, New York 10017

WILD AND
TENDER MAGIC

CHAPTER ONE

There it was again, this time in the kitchen window.

Abby Riordan stood at the edge of the woods, watching as the light where there should be no light flickered through the corner windows of the breakfast room. For a few seconds longer the eerie glow lingered, becoming more and more feeble as it shone from deeper within the house. Then the light was gone, leaving the windows to reflect the night, the panes dark and glistening from the rain that had fallen sporadically throughout the day.

It seemed obvious to Abby that the intruder must have left the kitchen area by the basement stairs.

As she moved away from the trees and started toward the house, Abby tugged her knit cap more snugly around her ears and pulled up the fur-trimmed hood of her parka.

It was late March, the ragged end of a very long winter. With today's thaw, the temperature had risen above the freezing mark for the first time in weeks, but with the coming of night the rain had turned to snow. Heavy, wet flakes were falling so thickly that Abby's footprints were obliterated before she had gone more than a few steps.

The veil of snow was so dense, it obscured even the

massive bulk of the Bauman house. The imposing Tudor-style residence was situated on the lakeshore, in the bowl of a natural amphitheater. It fronted on Butternut Drive and had all of Lake Mendota for its backyard. On summer nights the lights of Madison beckoned in sparkling pathways, like multicolored jewels floating on the surface of the water, but tonight the city had vanished into the snow. And even if it weren't snowing, the lake itself was frozen.

Deprived of the festive view of the city, Abby kept her eyes fixed on the breakfast-room windows. As the house loomed nearer she was increasingly vigilant for any sign of activity within. There should be none, for the owners, Ben and Peggy Bauman, had left for Florida shortly after Thanksgiving.

Although it had been Ben and Peggy's custom to winter in a milder climate ever since a heart attack had precipitated Ben's retirement five years before, this was the first year there had been any problem with break-ins.

It was true enough that the driveway had long since achieved notoriety as a lovers' lane. Abby used the drive to gain access to her own cottage, and on Saturday nights, weather permitting, she had counted as many as half a dozen cars parked along it. On several occasions she had also come across the litter of drinking parties on the grounds.

Then two weeks ago, during her usual Sunday afternoon visit, she had flushed out a group of teen-agers who had invaded the house. Evidently they had gone out the back door while she'd come in the front, because she had found a cigarette still smoldering in one of the overflowing ashtrays in the music room, and half-full beer cans were strewn about, bleaching white rings on Peggy's elegant mahogany-inlaid end tables.

Fortunately that was the worst damage the youths had done. There were many valuables in the house, but as far as Abby could determine, nothing was missing. Even the liquor cabinet was undisturbed.

She hadn't wanted to worry Ben and Peggy, but she'd felt obligated to report this incident to them. Their response had been to telephone from Bal Harbour and urge her to confine her inspection tours to the outside of the house.

"What about the plants?" she'd asked.

"To hell with the plants!" was Ben's gruff answer. "If it's common knowledge the house is vacant, it's dangerous for you to go inside on your own. You got lucky this time. All you interrupted was some local kids having a party, but Lord knows who you might surprise next time!"

"But the plants will die if no one waters them," she insisted. She knew how much Peggy prized her scheffleras and begonias.

"We'll work something out," Ben replied shortly. "Right now, all I want is your promise you won't go inside again."

Torn between her desire to reassure the Baumans and her need to find some means, however inadequate, of repaying them for their many kindnesses to Jamie and herself, Abby had been forced to concede to the logic of Ben's argument. She had given her word she would not enter the house even during the day, but when she'd seen the light, she had forgotten her promise. It was the reappearance of the small circle of illumination in the breakfast-room window that reminded her of it.

Halfway between the woods and the front door Abby came to a standstill. For the first time, it occurred to her that she might be wrong in her assumption. Perhaps tonight's unauthorized visitor was not simply another prankster. If the person with the flashlight was not a neighborhood youngster, it would be foolhardy to confront him inside the house. It could be dangerous to confront him at all.

She considered briefly whether it would be wiser to call the police. Then she squared her shoulders resolutely. The village of Maple Bluff was one of the most prestigious residential districts in Madison, and the most trouble-free. The governor's mansion was on Cambridge Road, only two blocks away. As a consequence, this area was especially well patrolled. Its crime rate was practically nil. In all probability tonight's intruder was one of the crowd who'd broken in before. Perhaps he was reconnoitering the possibilities of having another party, but it was likely he was relatively harmless. And if the intruder was only a juvenile, Abby had no wish to involve the police.

She knew most of the adolescent boys in the neighborhood. Some of them were Jamie's friends. They were lively, certainly, full of mischief, and given to occasional deviltry, but they were very definitely not hardened felons. If anyone were to catch one of them in the act of breaking and entering, she would rather it be her than the police.

Abby decided she'd honor her word to Ben by waiting outside until the intruder left the house. In that way she should be safe enough, and even if all she was able to do was identify the culprit, she could inform his parents. At that point they could take whatever action was necessary to put a stop to such pranks.

Keeping to the shadows of the shrubbery, Abby began working her way around the kitchen wing to the back of the house, paralleling the course the flashlight was charting.

It was rough going. She was breaking a trail through a winter's accumulation of snow, and with each step she took she sank into the drifts to a level well above her knees. When she saw the light was veering toward the library, she redoubled her efforts, for this seemed to support her theory that the trespasser was a teen-ager. In the previous break-in, entry had been gained by jimmying the

12

lock on the French doors leading from the library to the terrace.

She was nearing the house, following a windrow of young pine trees when, without warning, the light shone through the glass doors, sweeping over the terrace in a broad arc, as if the intruder had stumbled and dropped the light. It rolled to a stop quickly, coming to rest at an angle that projected its beam onto the upper branches of a tamarack only a few feet away from Abby, but not before the light had fallen directly upon her.

Her heart pounding in her throat, she stepped deeper into the shadow of the pines. Had she been seen?

Crouching down, she held her breath and tried to stop her teeth from chattering so that she could listen for some sign of activity from inside the library. At the same time she studied the ray of light.

It allowed her to see that one of the French doors was slightly ajar, but it also cut across the most direct path to the terrace. If she wanted a better view of the doorway, unless the intruder recovered the flashlight soon, she would have to make a detour to the far side of the pines in order to work her way closer to the house without making her presence known.

For several minutes Abby remained motionless. Whoever the intruder was, he hadn't yet retrieved the flashlight, and she wondered uneasily whether he might have injured himself when he'd fallen.

Finally her physical discomfort began to distract her. Her boots were packed with snow and her feet were so numb that she had no sensation at all in them. She wished she could stamp her feet a bit to warm them, but she didn't dare move for fear of being detected.

The silence was almost palpable, but Abby was not immediately aware of anything unusual about it. A few acres of private grounds separated the Bauman house from the road. Because of the sheltering belt of maples, it was always very quiet here, and tonight the stillness was even more intense because of the heavy snowfall. The sounds of traffic passing by on Butternut Drive were gradually deadened by the icy insulation. The silence was assuming an unnatural, expectant quality that became more disturbing by the moment.

It slowly dawned on Abby that something was terribly wrong. There was still no sign of movement from the house and she was concerned because the prowler hadn't picked up the flashlight. It was trained upon the tamarack, and snowflakes were swarming into its beam like moths attracted to a flame.

Nothing had changed, but all at once Abby was frightened. She straightened and tried to squeeze through the hedge of evergreens at her back. The branches were stiff and spiky, the pine needles crusted with a thin layer of ice. Her cramped muscles made it difficult to move, and when the hood of her parka snagged on one of the branches, she found herself trapped.

She frantically pulled off her mittens and attempted to untangle the material, but she succeeded only in creating a hopeless snarl.

At the crunching sound of footsteps in the snow, her struggles became even more frenzied. She was certain it was the prowler who was approaching and she clawed at the branches, fighting wildly to free herself.

The footsteps grew louder and her stomach knotted in fear.

Suddenly she knew the prowler was no high-school boy. She knew that he'd seen her, knew that she'd been duped into believing he had remained in the library when he'd actually left the house by the front door in order to corner her.

Dear God! What were his intentions if he caught her? And why had she taken matters into her own hands?

She was supposedly responsible, supposedly sensible.

14

But surely in such a situation any sensible person would not have hesitated over phoning the police.

Her racing thoughts galvanized her actions as one final question leaped into her mind: If something disastrous were to happen to her, what would become of Jamie?

Desperate to win release from the imprisoning clutch of the branches, Abby tore open the zipper of her parka and pulled her arms out of the sleeves. A mini-avalanche of snow cascaded into her shirt collar and sifted down her back as she bent the branches aside and forced her way between the pines, but she was beyond feeling anything but terror.

There was a pained exclamation from the prowler when she let go of the branches and they recoiled, slapping him a stinging blow across the upper chest and face. This accidental diversion allowed her to evade him, but she had covered a pitifully small distance before she heard him pursuing her.

Instinctively she ran toward the woods. In the wintry sanctuary of the maples, she might find some place to hide.

It was a strangely quiet chase. After his muttered oath when the branches hit him, the prowler maintained a stealthy silence. Any sounds his pursuit of her might have made were drowned out by the pounding of Abby's heart. She had no way of knowing whether he was gaining on her, but she sensed that he was.

She slipped and nearly fell. Her feet were weighted by the heavy snow and her lungs burned. If she could stop running long enough to catch her breath, even if only for a few seconds, perhaps she could think of some way to escape the prowler entirely.

Her terror had grown until it had become a living thing that dogged each step she took. It seemed to sap her strength instead of adding to it, so that the harder she tried to run, the farther away the maples appeared to be.

She risked a glance over her shoulder and saw that the

prowler was very big and frighteningly close, so close that even as she caught her first glimpse of him, he reached out and grabbed her by the scruff of the neck.

Again she managed to pull away, tearing her shirt in the process and leaving her assailant with nothing more than a raveled piece of fabric from her collar.

Fear spurred her to greater speed now, but just when she dared to hope that she might outdistance the prowler and gain the safety of the woods, he tackled her from behind, slamming her to the ground with a vicious lunge that knocked the wind out of her.

Stunned, her chest aching and her ears ringing from her impact with the ground, Abby lay where she had fallen, too dazed to offer further resistance. She was only vaguely aware that her assailant's body was pinning her down, pressing her so deeply into the snowbank that she was half buried. When at last he got to his feet and she was freed of his weight, she labored to fill her lungs.

"Okay, Junior, the fun's over."

Junior? A feeling of relief swept over Abby. He'd called her Junior! That must mean he thought she was a boy.

"Come on, let's have your name." His angry voice came from far above her. His speech was clipped, unaccented.

She was still unable to speak, and when she did not answer, he bent over her and searched the hip pockets of her jeans for some kind of identification. Finding nothing, he rolled her over, his hands rough and impatient.

She stared up at him, bewildered, as he slapped at the front pockets of her jeans. She couldn't see his face. All she could see was the dark outline of his powerful torso.

"Listen, you young hoodlum, stonewalling isn't going to help. If you don't cooperate with me, I'll have no choice but to call the police, so you might as well tell me your name."

The man's words might have been reassuring, but his tone was threatening, and her panic returned when he

16

continued frisking her, running his hands quickly over her legs and upward along her rib cage. He reached the sides of her breasts and, after an almost imperceptible hesitation, his hands closed over the soft mounds of flesh.

Although his touch was impersonal, air entered her lungs in a dizzying rush as she gasped with shock. For a moment the man froze, obviously puzzled.

"What the—" He pulled his hands away. "Who the hell are you?"

"A-Abigail Riordan." Her response was barely audible.

He stood erect, towering over her. "You're the Abby who lives in the guest cottage?"

"Yes." This time her answer was steadier. If he knew that, he must be acquainted with the Baumans.

"Sorry," he apologized brusquely.

Bending down again, he lifted her to her feet. He had dusted the snow from his car coat, and he would have helped her brush the snow off her clothing had she not stopped him.

"I can do it myself," she pointed out crossly.

"Sorry," he repeated. He didn't sound sorry. He sounded amused. "I thought you ran awfully funny for a boy. You're too soft for a boy too. I hope I didn't hurt you when I tackled you."

"Only my pride," she admitted stiffly. Actually she felt bruised all over and it was hard to keep from wincing as she dusted away the loose snow. Most of it was caked on, and now that she was more embarrassed than frightened, she was aware that she was very cold.

"What were you up to, skulking around the yard that way?" he asked.

"I saw your flashlight. I thought you'd broken into the house."

"Then why didn't you call the police?"

Trying to keep the shiver from her voice, she countered

17

warily, "Why didn't you turn on the lights instead of sneaking about in the dark?"

"The power's out. I suppose from the ice storm. At any rate, the line to the house is down. After I'd checked the circuit box, I was looking for a telephone so I could inform the power company."

"The phone has been disconnected."

"I didn't know," he replied curtly. "I'm Nick Gabriel, by the way."

"I hadn't realized you live in Madison," said Abby, testing him.

"I don't. I drove up from St. Louis."

"But your car—"

"I drive a pickup and it's in the garage," Nick cut in irritably. "I'd be happy to show you some ID, but it's too dark to read it."

"That's not necessary." Taking him at his word, Abby offered Nick her hand, almost gasping again when he took it. His clasp was firm, his hand large and warm, and the palm hard and calloused. It was very different from Gordon Sprague's smooth, well-manicured hands. Her breasts began to tingle where Nick had touched them, and she suddenly felt hot and confused.

"It's a pleasure to meet you, Mr. Gabriel," she said shakily. "Ben and Peggy have mentioned you often. They're very fond of you. You were married to—"

"That's right." Nick withdrew his hand abruptly.

The last of her fear had drained away and she realized that in her inane babbling she'd touched on what must be a painful topic for Nick Gabriel. His marriage to Ben and Peggy's daughter, Kirsten, had ended with Kirsten's tragic death only three years ago.

Wanting to ease the tense silence between them, Abby explained, "I thought you were one of the boys who broke in before. That's why I didn't call the police."

"I thought the same about you. Ben told me about the

18

problems you've been having with trespassers and asked if I'd house-sit for them."

"It's too bad they didn't fill me in on their arrangements. It would have saved both of us a great deal of trouble."

"They did telephone, but you were out. I believe they left a message with your brother."

"They told Jamie?"

Nick Gabriel nodded.

"I guess he must have forgotten to pass the word along." Dismay tinged Abby's voice at her brother's oversight. To compensate for Jamie's negligence and her own querulousness, she said, "Would you care to come along to the cottage? You can call the power company from there and let them know the line is down."

"Thanks," Nick accepted evenly. "I'll just take care of locking up and I'll be right with you."

CHAPTER TWO

Jamie Riordan could barely contain his excitement as he followed Abby into the kitchen of the guest cottage, leaving Nick Gabriel alone in the living room to make his phone call.

As soon as he and Abby were alone, Jamie asked, "Do you know who that is?"

"Of course I do," Abby replied. "Nick used to be Ben and Peggy's son-in-law."

"No, Abby, I mean besides that."

Jamie was usually so imperturbable that Abby's curiosity was aroused. Glancing up from the vegetables she was preparing to add to the roasting pan, she studied the thirteen-year-old. His thin young face was so flushed, he appeared feverish. It made her smile to see him so animated. As far as she knew, only one thing could provoke Jamie to such a display of enthusiasm.

"I recall Peggy mentioning he has something to do with baseball," she ventured.

"Something to do with baseball!" Jamie echoed, obviously appalled by her ignorance on the subject. "Jeez, Abby! That's like saying the Rolling Stones have something to do with music! Nick Gabriel was only the best pitcher in the major leagues, maybe the best since Koufax. It's for sure he was the greatest pitcher the Detroit Tigers ever had under contract. He won more than twenty games four seasons running. In the last year he played, his ERA was really fantastic—"

"Translation, please," Abby laughed.

"Earned run average," Jamie supplied. "The last season his was something like 2.42 and he recorded 206 strikeouts against only 77 walks and he had 5 shutouts, not to mention a no-hitter."

Abby stared at her brother, astonished that anyone who could rattle off so many statistics so easily should have forgotten to relay a simple message from the Baumans.

"Why do you use the past tense when you talk about his career in baseball?" she asked.

"He injured his knee a couple years ago while he was riding a motorcycle during the off-season. Anyway, he had to retire."

"I noticed he has a slight limp," Abby said. She wondered guiltily whether Nick's chasing her through the snow might have aggravated his injury. Before he'd tackled her, there had been no irregularity in his step. "But why should a knee injury interfere with his pitching?"

Before he could stop himself, Jamie groaned impatiently. He realized his sister didn't share his interest in sports any more than he shared her passion for music. She'd faithfully attended his Little League games, but he knew she'd been in the stands only because he was playing.

If the truth were told, he was grateful she didn't pretend an interest she didn't feel. If she had, he would have felt he owed it to her to do the same. What's more, except for one occasion when she had asked him why the players found it necessary to do so much spitting and scratching, she had never bugged him with questions about the game. But in the last few years she had taken him to watch the

Brewers or the Cubs play enough times that he couldn't understand how she could have remained so uninformed about one of the more salient points of baseball.

"Jeez, Abby, if you'd stop to think of the way a pitcher fires the baseball, the way he kicks and strides off the rubber with his pitching foot, you'd know how important his legs are. A pitcher has to use his whole body to deliver the ball."

Arrested by the image Jamie had evoked, Abby reached for another potato and absentmindedly began paring it while she considered how impressive Nick Gabriel must have looked in the close-fitting uniform baseball players wore.

He was tall and clean-limbed and his shoulders were broad and had what she thought of as an athletic slope, which she supposed was a result of superb muscular development. From his shaggy thatch of sunbleached hair to his size-twelve cleats, Nick would have looked every inch the athlete. Just the sight of him must have been worth the price of admission—devastating enough to make the hearts of the female spectators beat faster, and formidable enough to strike fear in the hearts of the opposing team.

Oh, yes! She could very easily imagine the power with which Nick could launch a baseball. She could personally testify that he was very strong. From the difficulty she was having making the slightest movement, she must have the bruises to prove it.

Jamie shook Abby out of her musings as he observed, "If you keep on peeling that potato, there's not going to be anything left of it." He helped himself to one of the carrots she had pared and bit into it. "Do you know how long Nick is going to be here?"

"I suppose until Ben and Peggy return from Florida. Evidently they asked him to house-sit for them."

"When do they plan on coming home?"

"They haven't said. You know they don't like to feel

22

they have to keep to a schedule, but if they run true to form, I'd guess they'll stay in Bal Harbour at least till early May."

Before she slid the roasting pan back into the oven, Abby offered Jamie another chunk of carrot. Lately his appetite was phenomenal. He was growing so fast that keeping him in clothes that fit even halfway decently put a strain on their budget. Just since the previous fall he'd grown a good six inches. Though he was now taller than Abby, she hadn't yet gotten used to having to look up at him.

Until a year ago there had been such a striking resemblance between the two of them that any stranger would have known at a glance they were closely related. Both of them had inherited their mother's finely modeled features and vulnerable mouth, and their glossy hair was an identical shade of sable brown. Their eyes were the same clear hazel too, but the expression in Jamie's was keenly perceptive while Abby's eyes were softened by secret dreams.

There were other differences as well. Jamie's hair was wiry and curly and Abby's had barely enough natural wave to fall into a smooth pageboy. They both had the sort of pale olive complexion that never burned or tanned, but Jamie had a few freckles while Abby's skin was as flawless as rich cream and so completely without undertones that it made her appear deceptively fragile.

Jamie's features had recently developed a new maturity, and his resemblance to his sister was becoming less noticeable. His face had lost its soft, babyish look and was assuming an unmistakably masculine cast that was all planes and angles. He had begun the metamorphosis into manhood, and only rarely now did Abby catch a glimpse of the little boy that made her want to hug him or to ruffle his hair.

She didn't often do that any longer. Jamie was very intolerant of overt expressions of affection from Abby. He considered them sappy and declared that since he was almost fourteen, he was too old for them.

Abby was a little less than twice that age. She was old enough to know that a person never outgrew the need for love, but she also knew that this was something Jamie would have to find out for himself.

With adolescent capriciousness, Jamie ran the gamut from being hypercritical to fiercely protective of her. *He* might find fault with her, but just let anyone else try it! In many small ways he demanded autonomy, yet in times of stress he still needed to be reassured that he wasn't totally independent. Sometimes he resented this. Sometimes he resented *her*. Mostly he took her for granted, which she supposed was very natural and an indication she hadn't done too bad a job raising her brother.

Abby smiled fondly at Jamie and saw that he had finished eating the carrots and was tearing open a packet of saltines.

"Is there anything else to munch on?" he asked.

"I think there's some cheese spread in the refrigerator."

Jamie found the cheese with a minimum of searching. Supplying himself with a knife, he made a row of crackers on the countertop and applied the spread so vigorously that he caused the saltines to rain a small shower of crumbs.

"Use a plate, please," Abby automatically requested. Glancing meaningfully at the number of crackers her brother was preparing, she teased, "Do you think that will be enough to keep body and soul together till dinner?"

"Ummm, I don't know," Jamie solemnly replied. "How long till it's ready?"

"An hour or so. I thought I'd get out of these damp clothes and have a shower."

"You do look kinda like a walking disaster area." Jamie eyed her critically. "You never did say how you got so wet."

24

"No, I didn't," she said in her firmest discussion-closed tone.

"Can I help with anything?" Jamie asked.

Surprised he'd heeded her wishes and not pressed her for more information, Abby answered slowly, "You could set the table for me."

"Okay," he agreed amiably.

After setting the oven timer, Abby started to leave the kitchen. She had reached the doorway to the hall when she was stopped by Jamie's voice.

"Abby," he called eagerly, "is it okay with you if I ask Nick to stay for dinner?"

So *that* accounted for Jamie's cooperative attitude, thought Abby. He'd been buttering her up, and he'd done it so deftly she hadn't even noticed.

For a moment she hesitated, then she asked herself, why not? The menu was simple, but the pot roast was certainly large enough to serve three. The company of an older man, especially an athlete of Nick Gabriel's stature, would be a treat for Jamie, and after driving all the way from St. Louis in such miserable weather, Nick might appreciate not having to go out to a restaurant tonight. All things considered, it was the least she could do.

Puzzled that she should have hesitated at all, Abby gave Jamie her permission.

She brooded over her uncertainty with regard to Nick while she was showering and changing clothes. It was unlike her to be indecisive, especially over such a trivial thing as a dinner invitation.

Gordon Sprague thought her tendency to make snap judgments was her worst fault. He had gone so far as to accuse her of being impetuous, but then he was so deliberate that he made everyone else seem rash by comparison. Furthermore, she hadn't needed him to call this failing to her attention. She knew that she was, by nature, a creature

25

of intuition and impulse, but until her mother's death this hadn't seemed a problem.

When Audrey Riordan died, Abby was barely eighteen and only the intervention of the Baumans had convinced the social workers to give Abby the chance to demonstrate that she was capable of caring for her five-year-old brother before they made other arrangements for him. That was when Abby had realized that if she chose to raise Jamie instead of allowing the court to appoint a distant relative of their father's as his guardian, she would have to grow up in a hurry.

After what was for her a lot of soul-searching, she had resolved that she would have to curb her impulsiveness, for she knew she tended to go off the deep end before she had determined whether she could hope to stay afloat. Then, more characteristically, she had fought with no holds barred for Jamie's custody and thrown herself wholeheartedly into making a home for him.

Since that time, somewhere along the way, she had learned to control her whims. Gordon's criticism was un-called for because, if anything, she had overcompensated. She had learned her lesson so well that the careful govern-ing of her impulses had become almost automatic.

Now she was so cautious that she routinely took time for second and third thoughts before she'd make a com-mitment. A few times she had anguished over major deci-sions, postponed making them until some golden opportunity had passed her by. Perhaps she was making that very mistake with Gordon. But that didn't mean she wasn't quick to form an opinion. She just tried terribly hard not to be swayed by first impressions.

As she stepped into a pair of trimly tailored white slacks, Abby tried to define her impressions of Nick, but the only thought that came to mind was that he was very strong. Her mirror told her that she'd been right about the bruises, and she removed a blue angora sweater from the

26

bureau drawer. Its long sleeves would conceal the darkening smudges on her arms. Hurriedly she pulled the sweater on and reached for her hairbrush.

Hadn't she overheard Peggy and Ben discussing something in connection with Nick shortly before they'd left for Florida?

She began brushing her hair, slowly at first, with long, smooth strokes, then more and more strenuously, so that her scalp tingled and her hair crackled with electricity under the assault of the bristles. Then she made a face at her reflection and tossed the brush disgustedly onto the top of the bureau.

Considering that he was so close to Ben and Peggy, she was surprised by how little she knew about Nick, but he seemed nice enough, which only made her uncertainty about him all the more mystifying.

She dug a silk scarf that matched the sweater out of the drawer and tied her hair back loosely at the nape of her neck. Still puzzling over her mental lapse, she left her room to join Nick and Jamie.

Guided by the sound of their voices, she found them in the living room, where they had set up the card table and were poring over the Scrabble board.

"Who're you trying to kid?" Jamie's forehead was wrinkled with consternation as he looked at Nick. "I challenge that one. I doubt there's such a word in *any* language."

"Challenge away," Nick dared him blithely. "It's a perfectly legitimate word."

Still muttering beneath his breath, Jamie picked up the dictionary at his elbow and began leafing through it. Its convenient placement attested to the number of times he'd referred to it in the past forty-five minutes.

Abby smiled at Nick as she approached the table. "Do you mind if I kibitz?"

"Kibitz, heck!" Jamie groaned. "What I need is reinforcements. I don't believe it, but it's actually in here.

27

K-U-M-I-S-S." He spelled out the word Nick had added to the board with his letter squares. Then with a sly glance at Nick, he said, "I'll bet you don't know what it means, though."

"You'd lose then, buddy," Nick retorted. "It's fermented mare's milk."

"Oh, yuk!" Jamie crossed his eyes at Nick. "Double yuk!"

Chuckling at her brother's antics, Nick turned to Abby. "Were you aware that Jamie is a cutthroat Scrabble player?"

"I ought to be. He beats the socks off me every time we play the game."

"Well, the socks are off the other feet now," said Nick.

With obvious insincerity, Abby remarked, "How sad."

Jamie was trying to keep a straight face. "Go ahead, you two. Gloat all you want. Pick on a poor little kid."

"Maybe Abby could give you a hand, Jamie," Nick offered. "I'm willing to take on the both of you."

"Big wow!" Jamie grumbled. "You're only about a million points ahead, and you want me to play the rest of the game with a handicap."

Nick laughed at Jamie's martyred expression while Abby tossed her head disdainfully and started toward the kitchen.

"Handicap, indeed!" she cried. "Since you feel that way, I wouldn't help you if you got down on your knees and begged me to, Jamie Riordan. Anyway, it's time to put the finishing touches on dinner."

"But, Abby, I'm starving. I thought everything was ready—that dinner only needed to cook for a little while longer."

"That's right, Jamie dear," she replied sweetly. "It's just that I forgot to sprinkle the rat poison on your pot roast."

There was an outburst of laughter from Jamie and Nick

at her threat, but as she left the room Abby heard Jamie say, "Jeez, Nick! I've added more words to my vocabulary in one hour of playing this game with you than I could in a whole semester of English classes."

During dinner Abby learned several things about Nick. She made her first discovery when she watched him fill his plate. His appetite was as huge as Jamie's. The second thing she discovered was that he'd won the Scrabble game, and the third was that he truly liked youngsters. He had already established an easy rapport with Jamie.

Usually Jamie was not very talkative with adults, but tonight was an exception. He fired so many questions at Nick that he didn't give either of them much chance to eat the food they'd piled on their plates.

When Nick had finished telling them about a recent personal appearance tour, Jamie said in an awed tone, "Golly! You must have been about *everywhere.*"

"I have traveled a lot," Nick replied. "But most of the time all I've seen was the inside of the local ball park."

"What's your favorite city?" asked Jamie.

"San Francisco," Nick answered without having to stop and consider the question.

"I've hardly been anywhere." Jamie sighed. "One of my friends went out to California with his parents last summer. His mom took a bunch of pictures while they were there, and do you know what most of 'em were of? Some dumb palm tree! Have you ever heard of *anybody* doing a thing like that?"

"Yes, I have," Nick replied soberly, respecting Jamie's indignation. "As a matter of fact, it's not all that unheard of for people from the northeast or midwest to flip out when they see their first real palm tree."

"Oh," said Jamie rather glumly. Then he brightened and asked, "So what's San Francisco like?"

"Hills everywhere, some so steep that you have to walk

29

or drive on them to believe they're real. The bay and the Golden Gate. Victorian row houses and Chinatown, Fisherman's Wharf and the De Young Museum—"

"I meant Candlestick Park," Jamie interrupted.

"Windy." Although his answer was succinct, Nick's eyes were crinkled with amusement at Jamie's eagerness. "Did you ever meet Joltin' Joe?"

"Joltin' Joe?" Abby spoke up, feeling she should make some contribution to the conversation. "Isn't he the one who used to play football? And for a while he did all those commercials for aftershave and panty hose?"

Jamie rolled his eyes toward the ceiling, and Nick barely suppressed a smile as he replied, "No, Abby. You're probably thinking of Broadway Joe Namath. Joltin' Joe is Joe DiMaggio."

"Oh, the 'Mr. Coffee' man."

From the look on Jamie's face, Abby knew he would have groaned again if Nick hadn't silenced him with a warning glance.

"That's the one," said Nick, "but he's also known as the Yankee Clipper."

Abby stared at Nick, as unenlightened as before. "If that was supposed to be a clue, it wasn't much help."

"He used to be an outfielder for the New York Yankees," Nick patiently explained, "and his nicknames refer to all the home runs he hit. He burned up the record books when he was playing with the old San Francisco Seals, and he hit .400 for the Yankees before he had an eye injury and fell back to .389."

Abby didn't try to enter into the conversation for some time after this. Jamie was monopolizing Nick's attention, inquiring if Nick had met various ballplayers—at least, she assumed they were ballplayers. She recognized none of the names. But when her brother asked what Babe Ruth was really like, she tried to cover a giggle with a cough.

30

Even she knew that Babe Ruth had played back in the 1920's.

Nick was taken aback by this question at first. "Babe Ruth was a little before my time," he began. Then he saw the mischief lurking behind Jamie's angelic expression and added, "I didn't know Abner Doubleday either." Laughing, he delivered a mock blow to the teen-ager's nose. "I'm glad you were putting me on," said Nick. "I was beginning to think I must have aged about fifty years since the last time I checked with a mirror."

"Babe Ruth," Abby said thoughtfully. "Isn't he the one who ran so funny?"

This innocent question sent Nick and her brother into gales of laughter. She looked from one to the other and back again, wondering what she had said that should cause such a reaction. Her confusion increased when Nick raised his water goblet to her and said, "You are absolutely right, Abby. Babe Ruth *is* the one who ran so funny."

When they finally stopped laughing, Nick and Jamie fell into a discussion of the merits of fastball pitching as opposed to styles that relied more on finesse.

"Did you ever throw a spitball, Nick?" asked Jamie.

"That's a question I've never given a direct answer to, but I'll make an exception for you, Jamie. The truth is that I never could learn to control a spitball well enough for it to be of any practical use."

"What's a spitball?" Abby inquired. "It sounds awfully—"

"Unsanitary?" Nick suggested.

"Actually I was going to say messy."

Nick grinned. "It's simply a catchall term that refers to any foreign substance a pitcher might introduce to a baseball."

"I always thought for sure your Staten Island sinker was a spitball," said Jamie.

"You weren't alone, Jamie. I was very careful not to correct anyone who made that assumption."

Their conversation became more and more technical. Each of them was bandying statistics about with great familiarity, and because it was so much Greek to her, Abby permitted her own attentions to stray.

Initially she was diverted by the way the light from the chandelier burnished the silver and gold streaks in Nick's hair and shadowed the strong bones of his face. Then she noticed his eyebrows. They were a little darker than his hair, and the line of one was broken by a small scar that pulled the arch slightly askew and lent a mildly sardonic slant to his features. His mouth was wide and mobile, and his blue eyes were unexpectedly intense and far-seeing, with tiny lines fanning outward from the corners as if he were accustomed to surveying vast distances.

She was drawn inadvertently into a comparison of the warm blue of Nick's eyes with the cool gray of Gordon's, and she decided that Gordon was more handsome than Nick. Although he was less blatantly masculine than Nick, Gordon's patrician good looks rivaled those of Richard Chamberlain, and Abby was accustomed to the envious glances other women cast in her direction when she was with Gordon.

Some of the cocktail waitresses she worked with at The Magic Lantern had told her they thought Gordon was very sexy. In fact, Ginger Fiore, whose husband owned the supper club, was the only person who had expressed disapproval of Gordon Sprague.

Abby had been dating Gordon for nearly three years. She had known him since high school, and she had always been aware of him. Yet, while his kisses and caresses were pleasant, Abby remained curiously unmoved. She had never even come close to losing control. Something— some basic spark, some kind of catalyst—was missing.

Gordon had been very patient with Abby. He'd never

tried to take greater liberties than she was prepared to grant, and she was grateful to him for being so considerate. He had told her he believed her reserve was a cover for deeper passions, and at first she'd believed him—probably because she wanted to so badly.

For a while she had thought her problem was that she knew Gordon too well, that she saw him more as a friend than as a lover. Lately, though, she had begun to wonder if there wasn't something missing in her fundamental sexual makeup. She had begun to wonder if she had any passion at all. . . .

With a start Abby applied a brake to her wayward thoughts, bringing them back to the present and feigning an interest in Nick's anecdote about one of his former teammates.

"So his speed didn't turn out to be much of an asset to him as a base runner," Nick was saying, "because Yancey never could learn how to slide."

As he concluded, Nick smiled directly at Abby and her breath lodged in her throat, for his eyes were bold with awareness of her and his smile was dazzling enough to eclipse the sun.

After she made this discovery, Abby found that she was watching and waiting for Nick to smile at her again, and each time he did, she felt the same delicious breathlessness. And although Jamie continued asking questions so that Nick was required to talk exclusively to him, Nick's eyes were speaking to her.

Finally, when the meal was finished and they left the dinner table to have coffee in the living room, talk turned from baseball to other topics. Inclining his head toward the piano that occupied a place of honor near the bay windows, Nick inquired, "Does one of you play?"

"Abby does. She's been playing ever since she was tall enough to reach the keys and she's really good. She can play the 'Minute Waltz' in fifty seconds flat!" Jamie proudly exaggerated.

Nick's glance drifted around the living room. The walls were maple-paneled, and the burnt-orange carpeting created a pleasant foil for the antique brass lamps and the oatmeal tweed of the upholstered pieces. There were no curtains or draperies at the windows. None were needed for privacy since this part of the cottage was sheltered by giant blue spruces which effectively screened it so that the guest house might have been in the midst of a forest rather than on its own small lot on the Baumans' property.

All in all it was a warm and charming room, but its dimensions were such that it was dominated by the piano, and the lack of draperies increased its resonance.

"It's not a concert grand, is it?" said Nick as Abby handed him his coffee cup.

"Nope, it's a size smaller," Jamie replied.

"Even so, its tone must be overpowering in a room this size."

"That all depends on the mood Abby's in. Sometimes, if she's ticked off, it about knocks me out of the house!"

Grinning broadly at Jamie, Nick reasoned, "There must be advantages in that."

"I guess so," Jamie returned doubtfully. "I mean, I'm never in the dark about whether she thinks I'm being a pain in the neck, but who can argue with a piano?"

"It's true, you know," Abby confessed, smiling wryly at Nick. "I do express my feelings at the keyboard."

"How about it?" Nick requested, returning her smile. "Would you play something for me?"

Her pulse was racing and she sipped her coffee, stalling for time before she tried to answer. "I—I'd be happy to," she acceded with only a slight stammer. Placing her cup on the lamp table, she rose and crossed the room.

While she was seating herself at the piano, Nick remarked off-handedly, "I've always regretted I didn't have the chance to learn to play a musical instrument when I was a boy."

"Jeez!" Jamie was horrified. "Don't let on to Abby you wanted to learn to play piano or she'll have you taking lessons so fast, it'll make your head spin."

"Sounds like yours is the voice of experience," Nick observed.

"Yeah," Jamie confirmed. "She tried to teach me even though I *hated* it."

"I take it, then, that you're not a music lover."

"Oh, music is all right." Jamie shrugged noncommittally. "It's just that I have better things to do with my time."

"He also has perfect pitch," Abby said dryly.

"And two left feet and ten thumbs," Jamie interjected.

"*And* an inclination to exaggerate," she countered. Her fingers wandered idly over the keys, striking a few dirge-like chords. "Now, aren't you going to tell Nick how long you were forced to continue your lessons?"

"Only a month," her brother slowly admitted. When Nick chuckled, Jamie added defensively, "But it seemed like it was a lot longer than that."

His woeful expression prompted Abby to play the opening bars of Mendelssohn's "Spring Song." The tune rippled out, offering an unsympathetic grace note to Jamie's sob story. Turning to Nick, he complained, "See what I mean? Who can argue with that?"

"If you'd continued your lessons instead of using the piano as a footstool, *you* could," said Abby.

"Okay, okay! I know when I'm outranked." Jamie threw up his hands in a gesture of surrender. "Besides, I have some homework to finish for tomorrow, so I guess I'd better hit the books."

Using a grip better suited to hand wrestling than to bidding a guest good night, Jamie shook hands with Nick. Before he left the room, he made a detour to Abby's side.

After planting a quick kiss on her cheek, he whispered close to her ear, "Thanks, Sis. Tonight was a gas."

Touched by his untypical display of affection, Abby watched Jamie until he had disappeared into the hallway.

"He's a thoroughly likeable kid," said Nick. "You've done a fine job with him."

"Thank you." She turned to look at Nick. He was sitting in the shadows and she had to strain to see his face, but she sensed that he was studying her. Her heart skipped a beat and she stirred uneasily, pushing one hand through the wisps of hair that had escaped the scarf to wave about her temples.

"I'm sorry I've been staring at you," Nick apologized, "but I expected you to be older."

"It's the name. People think of granny glasses and poke bonnets when they hear the name Abigail."

He laughed softly. "No, actually it was something Peggy Bauman said about Jamie only being five when your mother died."

"That's right."

"Then you must have been very young yourself."

"I was eighteen, but I had Ben and Peggy to help out if I got in a pinch or if I needed advice or anything. They were wonderful."

"They still are."

Abby nodded.

"What about your father?" asked Nick.

"He died before Jamie was born—even before my mother had told him about her pregnancy. He was killed in Southeast Asia."

"God, what a waste!"

For a time neither of them spoke, but their silence was companionable. After a few minutes had passed, Nick yawned and stretched tiredly.

"How about if I give you a hand with the dishes before I leave?" he suggested.

"That's all right," Abby demurred. "I'll take care of them later."

"Then how about the music you promised me?"

She indicated the music scores that were arranged on the bookshelves along one wall. "Is there anything you'd especially like to hear?"

"I'm fond of Chopin," Nick replied.

Without hesitation, Abby struck the first chords of the Nocturne in E Minor, and from the opening notes Nick was enthralled.

When he'd heard "Spring Song," his initial reaction had been an urge to laugh. Then, although Abby had played very little of it, he'd become aware that her rendition was intended to be humorous. Despite the hearts-and-flowers sentimentality of the piece, he'd recognized that her touch was crisp and light—almost ethereal—and her technique faultless.

He had been curious to see how she would interpret other compositions, but he hadn't anticipated the loving delicacy with which she captured the haunting melancholy of the nocturne.

The scope of her talent was more fully revealed when she followed the nocturne with a Chopin mazurka. He marveled at the artistry with which she controlled the tone of the piano, at the confidence with which she evoked the desperate, even driven, gaiety of the mazurka.

By no means did Nick consider himself an expert, but he'd attended enough concerts and recitals and listened to enough records that he felt he qualified as a knowledgeable fan, and it was his opinion that Abby was an awesomely gifted pianist.

A sharp twinge of pain in his injured knee caused Nick to swing his leg up onto the sofa. *Damn it,* he thought, *I should have slapped an ice pack on it right away.*

He stretched out until he was a little more comfortable, positioned to one side and slightly behind Abby. To take his mind off his discomfort, he concentrated on the soft shine of her hair in the lamplight, on the creamy curve of her neck, and on the perfection of the way in which it met her slender shoulders.

The pain gradually subsided and, relaxing against the sofa cushions, Nick closed his eyes. He stopped listening to the piano with a critical ear, stopped thinking, and gave himself over to experiencing the melody.

Abby continued to play and the music flowed around him, washing the last of the pain away.

CHAPTER THREE

The ringing of the telephone woke Abby the following morning. For a time after she opened her eyes she was confused by the gloomy light in the room. Judging by the semi-darkness, it couldn't be much later than six fifteen. The phone had been answered quickly, but Jamie couldn't have finished his paper route so early.

She peered drowsily toward the windows and saw that they were glazed with windblown snow. That explained the dusky light. It was later than she'd thought, and the caller must have been one of Jamie's customers or perhaps one of his friends.

She pulled the blankets over her head and buried her face in the pillow. She was almost asleep again when she heard the back door slam and the unmistakable sound of Jamie's footsteps coming into the house.

Her eyes flew open. If her brother hadn't been home to answer the phone, who had taken the call?

Throwing back the covers, Abby jumped out of bed and groped for her bathrobe. She ran to the door, opened it soundlessly, and stood motionless for a few seconds, listening while she fumbled into the sleeves of the robe and wrapped it about herself.

As was his habit, Jamie had turned the radio on. It was tuned to his favorite station, but above the snappy patter of the disc jockey, she could hear the low murmur of voices. Jamie was talking with someone and she was reassured by the cheerful note in her brother's voice. Then she inhaled the rich aroma of coffee. Her tension ebbed and she leaned against the door while she tied the robe about her waist. Yawning and rubbing the sleep from her eyes, she started groggily toward the warm pool of light that spilled into the hall from the kitchen.

It was not until she neared the kitchen that she recognized Nick's voice. Her step faltered as the first hazy recollections of the night before filtered to the surface of her mind. Never terribly alert first thing in the morning, she furrowed her brow, trying to remember.

Her memories returned in a rush and she was no longer the least bit sleepy. She was distressingly wide awake as she recalled that while she had been playing the piano at Nick's request, he had fallen asleep on the sofa.

She had tried to rouse him, and when she'd been unsuccessful, she'd tried to make him as comfortable as possible by removing his shoes and covering him with a blanket. After she had finished clearing the dinner table and washing the dishes, she'd tried to awaken him again, but he was still dead to the world. Finally she'd given up and gone off to bed.

Her knees were suddenly watery and she collapsed against the wall for support. *God,* she thought, glancing down at her faded pink flannel robe, *I must look a sight!*

Maybe she could sneak back along the hall to her room and change into something less disreputable. And put on some slippers, she hastily amended when she spied her bare toes peeking out from beneath the hem.

She had already taken the first step toward her bedroom, intending to carry out this plan, when Jamie called, "Abby? You okay?"

Groaning inwardly, Abby realized that it was too late. They'd already heard her.

"Yes, fine," she replied, hastily retying the belt of the robe more snugly about her narrow waist. Before she went into the kitchen, she combed her hair with her fingers and tucked it behind her ears.

When she entered the room, Nick's lips twitched, as if he were fighting an impulse to smile. He was seated across the breakfast table from Jamie with one foot propped on a chair. A sofa pillow cushioned his lower leg, and he'd strapped an ice pack around his knee. His clothes were rumpled from having been slept in, and an overnight growth of beard shadowed the cleft in his chin and emphasized the hard line of his jaw. But his blue eyes were bright and clear.

A prickly feeling between her shoulder blades told Abby that Nick was watching her every move as she walked to the counter where the percolator sat and poured a cup of coffee for herself.

"What was that big thud?" Jamie asked. "It shook the whole house. I thought you might have fallen."

Slowly, her mind scrambling for inspiration, Abby turned to confront Nick and her brother. "No, it was just that I—er, I bumped into the hall table."

Accepting her fib as the truth, Jamie returned his attention to finishing his breakfast. Around a last mouthful of cereal, he mumbled, "Gordon called."

"Did he leave any message?"

"He said he'd call again later." It was Nick who provided the answer to her question. He exchanged a conspiratorial glance with Jamie, which caused Abby to wonder uneasily what sort of confidences her brother might have divulged in her absence.

As if through some prearranged signal, the up-and-at-

41

'em voice of the disc jockey announced the half hour, and Jamie gulped down his orange juice, wiped his mouth with the back of his hand, and jumped to his feet, exclaiming, "I'd better get going or I'll miss my bus."

In keeping with his routine, he turned the radio off, and while he grappled with his jacket and the knapsack containing his schoolbooks, Abby took advantage of the distraction his leave-taking created and scurried to the chair he had vacated. She sank into it gratefully, hiding her bare feet beneath the skirt of her robe and smiling mechanically after her brother when he called "Catch you later" and let himself out of the house. At the last minute he paused in the open door, proclaiming, "If I was president, I'd abolish Monday morning!"

Struck by the blast of icy air his departure admitted, Abby shivered. She pulled her feet off the floor, hooking them around the bottom rung of the chair and tucking the folds of flannel around her toes. The cold draft curled about her ankles and crept up her legs.

The implications of Nick's reply began to sink in, adding to the chill until she felt numb all over. Her throat was dry, and she drank some of her coffee before she said to him, "*You* took the call from Gordon?"

Nick nodded. "I told him you were still in bed and he said he'd call again later. That was all."

"You told him I was still in bed," she parroted thinly, envisioning the conclusions Gordon would draw from that.

"Sorry about that," Nick returned steadily. "The phone woke me and I wasn't thinking too clearly or I'd have stopped to consider appearances and let it ring."

The sunny warmth of Nick's grin thawed Abby's reserve and she smiled back at him. All at once she was no longer concerned about Gordon Sprague. Maybe it wouldn't do him any harm to wonder how a strange man happened to be taking her early-morning phone calls.

"I'd like to apologize for falling asleep on you last night," Nick added. "I must have been more tired than I realized."

"That's quite all right," she replied, "only I hope you weren't too uncomfortable on the sofa. Is your knee—"

"It's better this morning." Nick brusquely turned her question aside to pursue the subject of Gordon. "Jamie tells me you're thinking of marrying this guy."

"Yes, I am. He proposed on Valentine's Day."

Nick's eyebrows shot up. "Why do you make that sound like an accusation? I'd imagine most women would find it pretty romantic."

"So would I, except that in Gordon's case it was so darned predictable. In this situation, for instance, he wouldn't be the least bit jealous," Abby said. "Or if he were, he'd never show it. He'd be very calm and tolerant."

Disconcerted by the wistful note that had crept into her voice, Abby got to her feet to refill their coffee cups. She was reminded of her lack of slippers when she stepped on a cornflake on her way to the counter. After a momentary hesitation she shrugged and thought, *What the hell!* Nick had surely seen bare feet before. It was senseless for her to be embarrassed or try to remain formal when he was sprawled in his chair as if he belonged there, completely at ease and matter-of-fact about their enforced intimacy.

In fact, her own frankness about Gordon had shocked her a little. Abby was by nature a rather private person, and, after all, she and Nick had just met last night. She reasoned that she hadn't had her second cup of coffee yet and was still too groggy to be thinking clearly. Or maybe it was Nick. He had been so easy to be with last night, so easy to talk to. It seemed very natural to be sitting across the breakfast table with him like this.

Then she scolded herself for trusting her instinctive response to this man so unquestioningly. She hardly knew Nick and was practically engaged to Gordon. And she

43

really hadn't meant to sound so critical of Gordon, so dissatisfied.

She carried the coffeepot back to the table and poured more of the hot, dark brew into each of their mugs. After she'd placed the percolator in the center of the table so that Nick could help himself if he wanted more, she sat down again and watched him add a liberal amount of sugar and cream to his. Usually she took her coffee black, but after the first swallow of her second cup, she recognized how strong it was. Wrinkling her nose, she stirred a spoonful of sugar into her own mug, sampled it, and found it a little more palatable.

She traced the rim of her mug with a fingertip and continued. "Don't misunderstand me, Nick. Most of the time I think that Gordon's predictability is an admirable trait. I feel very safe with him simply because he is so reliable. But there are occasions when it would be nice if there were some surprises left."

"In other words," Nick said bluntly, "he's boring."

Abby looked up at Nick, her eyes troubled and wide with inquiry. "Did I make Gordon sound like that? I shouldn't have, because he's really terribly nice."

"Abby"—Nick shook his head pityingly—"*nice* is for a lukewarm shower on a winter morning. *Nice* is for a pair of new shoes that hurt your feet but are too expensive to throw away. At best, it's a term I'd apply to a casual acquaintance. But *nice* is not the adjective I'd expect anyone to choose to describe a prospective marriage partner."

"You probably have a point there, but it's the truth nevertheless. And if I have difficulty expressing my feelings for Gordon, it isn't his fault. He's a good man. He's positively loaded with all the finer qualities. He's awfully conscientious, and he has a tremendous amount of integrity. I trust him implicitly. I respect him . . ." Recognizing how weak her defense of Gordon sounded, Abby trailed into silence.

"Liking, trust, and respect," Nick repeated pointedly. "And, oh, yes, admiration." He completed her list without inflection. "I'm no authority, but it strikes me that while all that might be the basis for a beautiful friendship, it would be a shaky foundation for a marriage."

"It goes without saying that I'm fond of Gordon," Abby hastily submitted.

"Fond?" Nick's expression was skeptical. "You're likely to discover that fondness is a poor substitute for love."

"But fondness can grow into love," Abby countered. "Besides, I'm not convinced love is as essential to a successful marriage as certain other things."

"Such as?"

"Basic compatibility, for one thing. My mother and father were very much in love, but in every other respect, they were totally wrong for each other."

"That's a mighty strong statement, Abby," said Nick.

"I know it is, but they had some mighty strong conflicts, so it's the only statement that applies."

"But they never divorced?"

Abby shook her head.

"Were they separated?"

"No, but—"

"In that case, who are you to judge them?"

Only an innocent bystander who was wounded in the crossfire, Abby silently retorted, but her vocal response was carefully neutral. "If you'll listen for a minute," she said evenly, "I'll try to explain. Then you can decide for yourself."

"Okay." Nick set his mug down on the table. "You have my undivided attention."

Abby was aware of that. Nick had propped his head up with one hand and was watching her the way he had last night, making a feature-by-feature appraisal of her face. When he looked at her mouth, she knew he was thinking about kissing her. And now his gaze was traveling lower, resting on her breasts.

Clutching the lapels of her robe high around her throat with one hand, she began to speak in a rush, without marshaling her thoughts.

"My father and mother were like oil and water. It seemed to me that they had only two things in common—both of them were hot-tempered, and neither of them had much of a sense of humor. That's another thing I really appreciate about Gordon—"

"You were going to tell me about your parents," Nick cut in, putting an end to her digression.

"Well"—she drew in a deep, calming breath—"Daddy was a pessimist. He hardly ever smiled and he never laughed. In a way, I suppose it was no wonder. He'd had it pretty rough. He was raised by an elderly uncle who was virtually a recluse, but he ran away from home when he was barely sixteen and enlisted in the army. After he was discharged, he worked his way through college. That's where he and my mother met. They always claimed it was love at first sight, but to soothe her parents' concern about their relationship, they waited to be married until Daddy had graduated and found a job."

"What kind of work did your father do?" Nick inquired.

"He was a journalist."

"Was he by any chance the Bruce Riordan who used to write for UPI?"

Although Nick had phrased the question casually, there was an undercurrent of excitement in his voice that Abby found puzzling. "Yes," she replied slowly. "That was my father."

"My God!" Nick exclaimed softly. "I cut my eye teeth on some of his columns. He wrote some classic pieces."

"Thank you," Abby acknowledged. "I'm very proud of him."

"You should be," Nick said rather sternly. "He's practically an institution!"

Abby was only mildly surprised that Nick was acquainted with her father's work. Bruce Riordan's assignments as correspondent for a wire service had sent him to trouble spots all over the world, and his vitriolic essays on the ugliness, violence, and corruption he'd witnessed in his travels had earned him a fair amount of recognition, especially among his colleagues.

What was astonishing, however, was Nick's admiration for her father's talents. Other people had praised him as highly, but such accolades usually came from fellow newspapermen.

Abby would have asked Nick about his familiarity with her father's reputation, but before she had the chance to question him, he pursued the subject of her parents.

"What about your mother?" he prompted.

"As I said before, my mother was the complete opposite of my father." Abby smiled affectionately at the thought of Audrey Riordan. "Where Daddy had been orphaned, Mother was her parents' only daughter. Granddad was a clergyman, and Granny Douglas was a bona fide southern belle, so Mother had been—not pampered, exactly, but doted on, sheltered. Daddy was the very epitome of the hard-bitten cynic, while Mother was an incurable optimist. She was devoted to taking on hopeless causes, not the least of which was trying to brighten Daddy's dark view of life. She was never terribly successful, of course, but she didn't let a little thing like failure get her down. She never lost her ideals, or her innocence. She was forty-two when she died."

"She sounds charming," Nick remarked softly.

"She was," Abby agreed. "Taken individually, both of my parents could be fascinating. They were people who had a lot to offer. But when they were together, each of

47

them was diminished. Whatever the reason, the combination just didn't work, and they tore each other to ribbons."

"What would they think of your marrying Gordon Sprague?"

"To be honest, I haven't given it much thought, but Gordon and I have a lot in common. We hardly ever quarrel, and he and Jamie get along very well."

Abby paused briefly. Her face was pensive when she went on. "So far, aside from the typical childhood ailments and some minor injuries, Jamie hasn't given me much cause for concern, but now that he's an adolescent, I worry that he'll need firmer discipline than I can provide. And—well, you saw him last night. I know he'd like having a man around the house. So I suppose the answer to your question is that my mother and father would approve of my marrying Gordon."

"Even though you don't love him?"

"I never said I didn't love him," Abby protested.

"You never said you did, either," Nick replied smoothly. "But maybe Gordon appeals to you, uh, physically."

"He's very good-looking."

Nick smiled. "That's not what I had in mind."

"No, I know what you had in mind." *It's just that I'm not sure about that,* she said to herself. Not sure, and afraid to say it out loud. She sighed and her eyes slid away from his. "For goodness' sake, Abby." Nick gave her a scoffing look. "You can't possibly be blaming yourself if Gordon doesn't make you feel . . . well, the way you think you should feel. You can't seriously doubt your own capacity for passion—not the way you play the piano! You're very talented, by the way. Have you ever considered playing professionally?"

"I do play professionally," she corrected him equably. "At the piano bar of The Magic Lantern."

"I meant concerts."

Abby shook her head. "I haven't the range for that."

Nick opened his mouth, preparing to disagree with her assessment of her ability, but she rushed on, declaring, "I don't say that out of false modesty or anything like that."

She held up one hand and spread the fingers wide. Bringing it close to her face, she studied it as objectively as if it belonged to someone else. It was a narrow hand, small but capable-looking, and beautifully proportioned. The nails were kept short and the fingers were long, fine-boned, and supple, with almost no tapering between the tips and the bases.

The truth was that her repertoire was restricted by the delicateness of her hands, and she had accepted her physical limitations long ago. She did well enough if she confined herself to certain composers: to Haydn, Mozart, and most of Brahms; to the tour de forces of Scarlatti; the Beethoven sonatas; the Chopin nocturnes. She even had a natural bent for jazz improvisation.

Inside her head, she could hear the powerful, crashing chords of Tchaikovsky's Concerto No. 1, the tranquil majesty of Grieg's Concerto in A Minor, the bittersweet dissonance of Liszt's "Funerailles," but she hadn't the strength to sustain her through an actual performance of such masterpieces. She just wasn't built for them.

"As you can see," Abby smiled ruefully as she held her hand out toward Nick, "my grasp of music exceeds my reach."

She almost gasped aloud at the electric sensation she felt when Nick reached across the table and caught hold of her hand with both of his. Rotating it from back to palm, he looked at it thoughtfully and measured it against his much larger hands.

She watched as if mesmerized while he curled and straightened her fingers several times, play   with her hand absently, drawing teasing patterns over   ⁓ following the delicate veins to her wrist.

Tearing her gaze away from their joi

registered that he was saying something to her, but she was so distracted by the feather-light touch of his fingers that she heard only the words, "How about it?"

"P-pardon me. I'm afraid I wasn't paying attention."

With a gentle tug of his hand on hers, Nick brought her to her feet. Another tug propelled her to his side of the table, and a third pulled her down so that she was seated on the hard bench of his thighs with his arms around her waist.

Smiling lazily into her eyes, Nick said, "I asked if you'd be interested in conducting a simple experiment to prove it's not any fault of yours if Gordon doesn't turn you on."

"An . . . an experiment?" she whispered uncertainly, tensing for escape. "I don't—"

"Trust me." He brushed her lips with his, silencing her. "I guarantee it will be painless."

Her stomach seemed to be doing flipflops and her pulse was hammering erratically. She couldn't seem to look away from the sensual curve of his mouth.

She was vaguely aware that one of his hands had left her waist to travel upward along her spine. It wove its way through the silky tangle of hair at the nape of her neck and cradled her head to prevent her turning away while he outlined her mouth with quick, tantalizing kisses. She felt her own lips tremble with anticipation before he finally claimed them fully with his.

His mouth was warm and soft as velvet. He compelled her response, yet he maintained a certain restraint, purposely not rushing her, not asking for more than she was willing to give.

Dear God, what would Gordon think if he found her this way? She was being horribly disloyal, and she should put a stop to this right now, before it was too late.

But it was already too late. Her senses were reeling and she had relaxed against Nick's chest so that her body was ~urving fluidly, conforming to the hard angles of his.

She pulled away from him far enough so that he could see her bemused face and he asked, "What do you say? Shall we continue the experiment?"

Even as she thought, *You're a fool, Abigail Riordan, if you go along with him,* Abby heard herself reply, "Carry on, Dr. Gabriel."

For a moment more he looked at her. Then he smiled, and his smile left her breathless even before he began to kiss her again. This time the pressure of his mouth alternated between gentle insistence and hard demand until she responded to the erotic play of his lips and tongue, wildly returning his kisses.

Awash with sensation, she remained on his lap, her arms hanging limp at her sides. She was utterly incapable of moving and, of necessity, Nick held her more closely, his arms hugging her to him to give her support. By the time he freed her mouth, she hadn't the will to move. She couldn't even manage to open her eyes all the way when he abandoned his exploration of her mouth and his lips trailed across her cheek to her temple.

"Did Gordon ever make you feel this way?"

"I'm not sure," she murmured dreamily. A mischievous sparkle danced in her half-open eyes. "Maybe if you kissed me again, it would help me decide."

"Abby!" Nick's arms tightened about her. His intonation of her name hovered somewhere between a groan and a sigh. "You're very sweet, but you sure know how to hurt a guy."

Her eyes opened wide with concern and she pulled herself erect. "Your knee!" she cried.

"It's not my knee that's bothering me." Nick smiled sardonically when he saw the dawning recognition in her eyes.

Suddenly conscious of his arousal, Abby leaped to her feet. She took a few shaky steps away from him before she came to a stop, standing with her back to him, her head bowed, trying to think of some means of making a graceful retreat from the kitchen. Her face felt as if it were on fire.

"Abby." This time Nick said her name so softly that it sounded like an endearment. "Does Gordon drive a green Chevy with a white vinyl top?"

Her head snapped upright. "How in the world did you know?"

"I didn't, but a car matching that description just turned into the drive."

Abby was too stunned to comment on this information. After a hasty glance confirmed that it was indeed Gordon's car, and that it was already creeping over the little wooden bridge where Butternut Creek crossed the property, she walked unsteadily to her chair and sank into it.

Using the chrome-plated coffeepot as a mirror, she tried to smooth her hair. Her hands were shaking, and although the rest of her face was pale, her cheeks were vivid with color.

"Here," Nick said gruffly, offering her his pocket comb.

She accepted it gratefully and began working it through the worst of the snarls. Leaning closer to her makeshift mirror, she lamented, "I can't remember the last time I blushed, so why do I have to do it now, of all times?"

"Gordon has been remiss in his attentions to you if you don't even know a blush from a whisker burn." Grinning mockingly, Nick paraphrased, "Fickleness, thy name is Abby!"

Rankled by this taunt, Abby tilted her chin proudly. "That's not fair—"

"Oh, isn't it?" Nick persisted. "Look at yourself! Your lips are still warm from my kisses and all you can think of is preparing to meet another man."

"It's not that," she protested. "It's only that I don't want Gordon to think that we were—that we were—"

"Doing what we might have been doing if I hadn't called a halt?" Nick's smile faded. "Well, why the hell not? From all indications, Gordon could use a good shaking up."

Nick got to his feet and limped to the window and stared moodily out into the snowy backyard, watching as Gordon's sedan pulled into the parking area behind the house.

"Please, Nick, try to understand," Abby pleaded. "What happened between us just now was a mistake. I know I've given you the wrong impression, but I'm very fond of Gordon, and he's been so kind to Jamie and me. I don't want to hurt him."

Pivoting away from the window, Nick strode to Abby's side and pulled her to her feet.

"I understand better than you realize," he said crisply. "And I'll behave like a gentleman to your boyfriend. But in return, you have to do something for me."

"What's that?" she asked tremulously.

Nick's hands moved from her shoulders, slipping downward to cover her breasts, gliding inside her robe to fondle the rounded warmth within. His eyes were hooded as he looked down at her, gauging her reaction as he fingered the nipples, teasing them to tautness.

"Admit that he never made you feel the way I can," he commanded harshly.

Abby knew that she was genuinely blushing now. Powerless to stop him, she could feel her cheeks flaming with embarrassment as she weakly nodded her agreement.

When Abby opened the back door and saw that Gordon was, as usual, a model of suave urbanity, a comment Merle Halloran had made a week or so before popped into her mind.

One evening when Gordon had come into The Magic Lantern, Merle had stopped at the piano bar on her way to deliver his drink and whispered, "I don't know about you, Abby, but I'd like to run my fingers through that gorgeous blond hair of Gordon's, and loosen his tie, and mess him up a little." As an afterthought Merle had sighed lustily and admitted, "What I'd really like to do is mess him up quite a lot!"

This morning Gordon's tidiness made Abby even more self-conscious about her own unkempt appearance. She felt miserably guilty as she confronted him.

He stood in the doorway, tall and slender and elegant. In spite of the brisk wind that swirled around the cottage, his hair was impeccably groomed, and his smooth, tanned face was glowing with good health and the frigid morning temperature.

One of the things Abby liked about Gordon was that he wasn't vain about his good looks. But while his physical appearance was something he accepted as a natural result of genetics, he looked upon his robust health as a sacred trust. He was fond of saying that the body was a temple that must be zealously guarded, and he practiced what he preached. Nothing short of a major catastrophe could disrupt his daily regimen, which included a half-mile swim at the university pool and twenty minutes under a sun-lamp.

He ate only wholesome, organically grown foods, and he deplored Abby's occasional junk-food binges. One of his favorite adages was "You are what you eat," and she'd lost track of the number of times he had lectured her about her sweet tooth. But he had stopped nagging her after the time she'd replied flippantly, "If that's true, I'd rather be a jelly doughnut than a bowl of alfalfa sprouts."

Maybe there was something to his theory about nutrition, though, because his appearance was so nearly perfect that Ginger Fiore had once inquired, "Doesn't it get to be a drag, Abby, going out with a man who's prettier than you?"

When he came into the kitchen that morning, Gordon smiled warmly at Abby, but his eyes became faintly hostile as they darted over her head and found Nick.

"Sorry to stop by unannounced at such an early hour," Gordon apologized, "but I was concerned about you, Abby, dear. Is everything all right?"

"Everything's fine, Gordon."

Abby detested Gordon's calling her Abby, dear, but she returned his smile. When she saw that Nick had removed the ice pack, resumed his seat at the table, and was lounging back in his chair as if he owned the place, she glared disapprovingly at him.

"This is Nick Gabriel." She introduced them with some reluctance.

Nick got to his feet. "We've met," he said evenly. "We introduced ourselves when we talked on the phone."

The two men approached one another warily and exchanged a perfunctory handshake.

"I've heard a lot about you, Sprague," said Nick.

"And I've *read* a lot about you," Gordon countered.

"But only in the most scholarly publications," Nick suggested, tongue-in-cheek.

"I genuinely dislike shattering whatever preconceived notions you might have about me, Mr. Gabriel, but when I'm waiting in the checkout line at the supermarket, I must confess that I do read the odd tabloid."

"I'll just bet you do."

The cool derision in Nick's voice made it clear that his comment had not been intended as a compliment, but before the antagonism between the men could escalate any further, Abby hurriedly interjected, "Why don't you take your coat off, Gordon, and go on into the living room while I make some fresh coffee for us."

"Don't bother on my account," Gordon declined stiffly. "I can't stay more than a few minutes."

"And I should be getting back to the main house. The power company said they'd send someone out first thing this morning," Nick said. He started toward the front door, but when Abby automatically began to follow after him, he stopped her, saying, "You don't need to show me out. I know the way."

In the archway that led to the dining alcove, Nick abruptly turned to face them and deliver his parting salvo. "Thanks for last night, Abby," he said softly. "You were wonderful."

The warmth of Nick's smile and the fiery blue of his eyes rendered Abby speechless, for they hinted, untruthfully, that she and Nick had shared an evening of rapturous intimacies. The angry intake of her breath underscored the innuendo, but before she could think of a suitably cutting reply, Nick was gone and she was left alone with Gordon, who was studying her speculatively.

When the front door had closed behind Nick, Gordon asked quietly, "What happened here last night?"

"Nothing."

"I see." He nodded skeptically. "If you don't want to tell me—"

"There's nothing to tell!" she insisted hotly.

"Very well, Abigail, if you say so. I only hope you haven't permitted your emotions to cloud your better judgment. Nick Gabriel is not the most savory character."

It was apparent to Abby that Gordon didn't believe her, that he was merely humoring her, and this infuriated her all the more.

"What do you mean by that?" she asked shortly.

"Surely you must have read about his run-in with the law! I'm afraid some of the details elude me, but I do recall that he was caught red-handed trying to smuggle narcotics into the country."

Sickened more by the triumphant gleam in his eyes than by what he'd told her, Abby turned away from Gordon and strode restlessly to the window. In an effort to control her temper, she counted to ten and concentrated on the winter scene outside. The snow had stopped and a watery sun was peeking through the clouds, casting pastel shadows on the drifts of white.

"I can see you don't want to believe he's capable of such a thing—"

Wondering at the firmness of her conviction, she interrupted, "I'd put it more strongly than that, Gordon. I *don't* believe it."

"Abby, Abby, Abby." His repetition of her name was condescending. "I appreciate your reluctance to think the worst of anyone, but I hope you'll heed my advice and keep your distance from this Gabriel fellow."

"And I appreciate your concern, but I think you're overreacting. Ben and Peggy Bauman trust Nick. They've even arranged for him to take care of their house till they return from Florida."

"That may be so," Gordon grudgingly conceded, "but where there's smoke there's fire, and the fact remains that he's under indictment for possession with intent to sell narcotics."

"I thought that in this country a person is supposed to be presumed innocent until they've been proven guilty!"

Gordon sighed resignedly. "Well, I've warned you anyway. I know how determined you can be once you've made up your mind about something. It's just that when I spoke to Gabriel on the phone earlier, I decided the least I could do was caution you about him."

Now that the discussion about Nick's alleged crime seemed to be at an end, Abby looked at Gordon curiously. "Why *did* you call?" she asked.

"I had a bit of good news to share with you. You remember that last fall I applied for an opening as head of the Sociology Department at Dryden University?"

Abby nodded.

"It had been so long since I'd heard from them, I assumed the job had been filled, but yesterday evening I received a telephone call from the outgoing chairman.

They want to interview me." He glanced at his wrist-watch. "And I see that if I don't get going, I'll miss my flight. I only stopped in on my way to the airport."

"I'm very happy for you, Gordon." Abby smiled to show she harbored no hard feelings because of his unsolicited advice. "I hope the interview goes well."

"Thank you for the sentiment, but if you really care whether my trip is a successful one, you'll give me your word you won't see Nick Gabriel while I'm on the West Coast."

Her eyes flashing rebelliously, Abby opened her mouth to reply, but Gordon gave her no chance to speak. "Look here, Abby, dear, it's only till the end of the week," he reasoned blandly, "and I can hardly be expected to be at my best if I'm worried about you."

And he calls me stubborn! Abby thought. Her sweetly rounded chin tilted to a defiant angle, and the soft curve of her lips hardened to a grim line, but her response was almost inaudible.

"You needn't worry about me," she whispered.

She had evaded giving Gordon the promise he'd demanded, but he chose to take her statement as reassurance that she would avoid Nick.

Although Gordon believed he knew Abby well, he had never noticed that whenever she was angry, her voice deserted her. She might shout with joy along with the best of them, but if she was annoyed, her vocal cords seemed to atrophy. Sheer rage had always left her nearly mute.

Gordon gave her a chaste kiss before he left. "Thanks so much, Abigail," he said. "I'm very relieved. I'll call you when I get back."

"Do that," she choked, but Gordon's smug expression had fanned the flames of her resentment so that she was unable even to whisper, and he didn't hear her.

CHAPTER FOUR

Although she looked several years younger, Abby was twenty-seven. Most of her old school friends had been married for years and quite a few of them had already started their families. But unless one counted the pledge of matrimony that was made to Abby by a six-year-old classmate when she was in first grade, Gordon's was her first proposal.

When she was a teen-ager, her all-consuming interest in the piano had precluded much dating. Then, when Jamie was small, she hadn't liked leaving him with a sitter any more than was necessary. Besides, she'd had to concentrate on earning their living, so she hadn't had much free time.

It wasn't until Jamie had become more self-sufficient and she'd found her present job that she had begun to feel there was something missing in her life.

Admittedly, her experience with men was limited, but when she thought about it, it seemed that most of the unmarried men she'd known fell into one of two categories.

In the first group were the cerebral types she'd met

because of her involvement with music—at concerts and recitals and through her connections with the university. In the second were the more libidinous types she met through her work.

While The Magic Lantern wasn't a singles' bar and the majority of men who came in were accompanied by their wives or dates, they did get their share of customers who were on the make.

Ginger Fiore had an apt description for these men. "They're about as original as if they'd been turned out by the assembly line at Mattel," Ginger stated drolly. "They seem to think it's sexy to walk without moving their hips and talk without moving their lips."

At any rate, they made it fairly obvious that their only interest was in finding a temporary playmate, so even if it hadn't been a matter of policy that employees were not to socialize with the patrons, Abby wouldn't have felt any inclination to go out with one of them.

Maybe she was a poor judge of character, or maybe it was just her bad luck, but the men she had dated in the last few years seemed to lose interest in her as anything other than a prospective bed partner as soon as they discovered she was responsible for her brother. She'd had more than a few propositions, but no proposals. Until Gordon's.

If she'd had only herself to consider, this wouldn't have mattered, she thought, but there was Jamie to think of.

Gordon and Jamie would probably never be terribly close, but they got along well enough, and Gordon could certainly exert the male influence Jamie needed.

Abby had never deluded herself that she was in love with Gordon, but since she'd never been in love with anyone else, she might not have recognized it if she had been.

Anyway, as she'd told Nick, her parents had supplied ample evidence that love was no guarantee of a happy marriage. Her father had been home only for short periods between assignments, but whenever he'd been present, their house was transformed into a battleground. One of her earliest memories was of lying in her darkened bedroom late at night while her mother and father had fought what sounded like World War III in the living room. She had unsuccessfully tried to muffle the sound of their angry voices by hiding her head under the bedclothes.

Abby didn't know what her parents had fought about before she'd come along, but after her birth most of their arguments revolved around her or around her mother's longing for another child. Audrey had wanted a son, but Bruce Riordan believed it was the worst kind of folly to bring children into a world that might incinerate itself at any moment. He'd thought it was criminal that they'd had Abby.

In spite of the ongoing conflict with her husband, in spite of her frustrated maternal longings, Audrey Riordan had persisted in seeing nothing but the silver linings while Bruce saw only the clouds. Even when she'd learned she was pregnant with Jamie, Audrey worried very little about how her husband might react to the news. She'd had enough trepidations that she had postponed telling him about the baby, but her faith in her happily-ever-after philosophy was unshakable.

Abby sometimes felt that she had inherited equal measures of her parents' respective natures. No matter how she struggled to find the middle ground, occasionally she vacillated between idealism and cynicism.

A perfect example was the time the previous summer when Gordon had taken Jamie and her to the state fair in Milwaukee. They'd spent the morning touring the exhibits, and in the afternoon they'd attended a rock concert by one of Jamie's favorite groups. After dinner Jamie had suggested they visit the carnival, and while they were strolling down the midway, they'd stopped to watch one of the barkers, who was performing feats of magic.

Abby was spellbound by his skillful sleight of hand, but Jamie and Gordon were not as willing as she was to be deceived. The barker was in the midst of a particularly intriguing trick when Jamie suddenly pointed out the mirrors he'd used to create the illusion.

"Look!" Jamie exclaimed. "I see how it's done."

"You're very astute, Jamie." Gordon praised the boy, impressed by his cleverness in spotting the mirrors.

Much to the barker's relief, Jamie and Gordon had wandered away from the concession, but Abby stayed behind for a few minutes. She knew she should have been proud of Jamie, but she had bitterly resented his exposing the fraud. Sometimes reality was painful, and it was better if it was softened. Sometimes she preferred to believe in magic.

Now, because their disagreement over Nick had shown Gordon in a new and less than flattering light, she had to try extra hard to be realistic about him.

She told herself that, Nick's opinion notwithstanding, affection and common interests weren't such a bad basis for marriage. She told herself that Gordon was a decent, honorable man. If he was a bit stuffy, if now and then he could be sharply critical, he more than compensated for these faults by being sweet and considerate so much of the time.

Besides, she was far from perfect herself. If Gordon wasn't the romantic lover of her dreams, the fault was hers. The longing to be swept off her feet was only a foolish fancy after all; there was no such thing as an unmixed blessing.

In the week of Gordon's absence, Abby very nearly convinced herself that all this was true. Then, on Saturday night, Gordon phoned to let her know he was back in town. The first thing he asked was whether she'd seen

Nick again, and her reservations clamored to the forefront once more.

"No, Gordon," she replied evenly. "I haven't seen Nick." Her answer was honest as far as it went, but she didn't tell Gordon that this was more by accident than design. Instead, she asked, "How was your trip?"

"Super, Abby, just super!" He made a dramatic little harumphing noise and announced, "You, my dear, are speaking to the new chairman of the Sociology Department of Dryden University."

"Oh, Gordon, how marvelous! Congratulations! I'm so very happy for you."

"I knew you would be."

"What's Dryden like?"

"It's a fairly new campus, so all of the buildings are of the same architectural design. They're all redwood and glass and very modern. The campus overlooks the ocean, and I must say it's a magnificent setting. Considering the size and relative newness of the college, the library is quite extensive, but what impressed me most is that the ratio of students to faculty compares favorably to the University of Wisconsin. Oh, and the people I met were most congenial. Dr. Beddoes, the outgoing chairman, was helpful above and beyond the call of duty." Gordon paused briefly, and when he spoke again, his voice was heavy with meaning. "You realize that this means I'll be leaving Madison at the end of May, don't you, Abby?"

"Of course I do, Gordon," she replied quietly. "You must be looking forward to the move. Dryden sounds as if it's all you've hoped it would be."

"It is, my dear. But what have you been up to while I've been away?"

"Not a heck of a lot. The weather was so bad early in the week—"

"I heard about the spring blizzard," he said in a dry voice. "Would you believe the temperatures were in the sixties out on the Coast? It rarely drops below freezing there."

"Oh, *stop!* I can't stand it! And you have to rub it in," Abby laughingly complained. "Lately I've wondered if this winter is *ever* going to end."

"You sound a little hoarse, Abby."

"Well, I've had the flu the last few days."

"Oh, goodness . . . I'm sorry to hear that, dear."

By now Abby was convalescing. She was feeling a little lonely, even fretful, in her isolation. But Gordon had such a hangup about being exposed to illness that when he offered to stop in and see her over the weekend, she said she'd rather he didn't. They did make a date for the next Wednesday afternoon, however. That was the first weekday he had free.

Coward that she was, Abby was relieved not to have to see Gordon just yet. She sensed that he intended to press her for an answer to his proposal, and for all her agonizing over it, she still wasn't sure how she should answer him.

And her conscience bothered her because she hadn't told him that Jamie had taken to spending most of his waking hours with Nick. Her brother had developed such a strong case of hero worship that his conversation was peppered with his idol's name. Jamie was ecstatic because Nick not only welcomed his company, he had also invited him to work out in the gym Ben had installed in the basement of the main house.

Since Gordon had mentioned that Nick had been arrested on narcotics charges, Abby realized the prudent thing to do would be to keep Jamie away from him, but the more she thought about it, the more convinced she became that Nick couldn't possibly be involved with trafficking in illicit drugs. If she'd had any unresolved doubt about this, the recollection of his clear eyes and open smile would have banished them.

She hadn't the heart to raise any objections to Jamie's

daily visits to Nick, but she had no wish to revive the controversy over the man, especially when Gordon was in such rare high spirits about his new appointment.

By Tuesday, Abby felt well enough to return to her job. She enjoyed her work and she was inordinately fond of The Magic Lantern, which had begun life in the 1930's as the lobby of a movie palace. In renovating the building, the Fiores had preserved the Moorish architecture and capitalized on the plush maroon-and-gilt interior to the extent that the restaurant was trendy and high camp.

In keeping with its name, the walls of the cocktail lounge were papered with a design of old movie posters and lined with autographed black-and-white photographs of celebrities. The photos were placed in order of importance, with the pictures of those who were less well-known consigned to the dimly lighted corners at the rear of the long room.

The piano bar itself consisted of a shiny black lacquered baby grand flanked by large potted palms which, through some cunning trick of lighting, were made to appear twice as lush and exotic, and the bar itself.

Abby had hoped working might take her mind off the troublesome inability to come to a decision about Gordon, but it didn't. March was roaring out like a lion and a freezing rain was falling. As a result, it was a quiet night at The Magic Lantern, even for a Tuesday.

Usually she played from six in the evening until the cocktail lounge closed at one A.M., but by eleven o'clock, except for the staff, the restaurant was deserted and the bar very nearly was. Even Harlan Crowley, an elderly gentleman who came in several times during the week to hear Abby play, hadn't shown up. At midnight Tony Fiore sent Abby home.

She slept very little that night, and the following morning she found that her uncertainty affected the smallest everyday choices she had to make.

"You look awful!" Jamie informed her bluntly when she wandered into the kitchen to see him off to school. "Are you sure you're not having a relapse or something? Maybe you should go back to bed."

"I'm all right," she insisted, but her preoccupation was apparent to her brother.

She filled the percolator with water and measured some coffee to put into the basket. Then she forgot to put the basket in the percolator before she plugged it in, and Jamie had to call her oversight to her attention.

She poured cereal into a bowl and absentmindedly ate most of it before she realized it was a brand she hated. Scowling, she pushed the bowl away.

Only then did she notice that Jamie was studying her, his young face sober with concern.

"Are you sure you're okay, Sis?" he asked. "I could stay home from school today if you're not."

Striving for normalcy, she replied lightly, "I appreciate the sacrifice, but it isn't necessary. I'm fine."

Not entirely reassured, Jamie left for school and Abby returned to her bedroom to get dressed for the day. Clad only in her underwear, she stood in front of her closet, unable to decide what to wear. Finally she grabbed a heather plaid skirt and matching sweater, simply because they were the first things that came to hand.

She managed to get through the routine housework easily enough, but later that morning, when she went to the supermarket to restock their empty cupboards, the crippling uncertainty struck again.

As she pushed her shopping cart past the checkout counters, she caught sight of the tabloids that were displayed nearby, and the headlines in one of the newspapers leaped out at her. In banner captions it heralded the latest scandal about some aging actress. The accompanying photo was unflattering, to say the least, and Abby found the entire effect quite disturbing. Nick's name and photograph had probably been splashed across that gossip sheet not too long ago, she thought. Hadn't Gordon even mentioned it the other morning? Nick had seemed so unruffled at the time and Abby felt sorry now for anyone who had lived through such publicity.

Pursued by this reminder of Gordon and of her quandary, she headed for the meat area. She was floundering mentally, peering into the refrigerator case without actually seeing the array of steaks, chops, and roasts, when Nick found her.

Touching her arm to rouse her, he observed lightly, "I know prices are high, but you've been staring at the ground round as if you expect to be charged just for looking at it. Is something wrong?"

Abby smiled brightly to allay his suspicions. "I was just wondering what Jamie might like for dinner."

"You certainly are conscientious," Nick said dryly. "You haven't moved for the last ten minutes."

"Has it really been that long?" she asked shakily.

"Just about, and since it's such a problem, I'll make it easier for you by inviting you and Jamie to have dinner with me this evening."

"I'd like that, but I can't tonight. I'm working."

"Lunch then," Nick suggested.

Abby's initial impulse was to yield to temptation and accept, but in the next instant she was assailed by doubt. Her plaintive sigh telegraphed her hesitancy, and Nick took command.

With one arm around her shoulders, he propelled her away from her still-empty shopping cart and out of the store.

"What about your shopping?" Abby belatedly protested, her feet dragging to a stop as the electric-eye doors closed behind them. "What about mine?"

"We'll come back afterward and do it together," Nick answered, his hand at the small of her back urging her forward.

Thirty minutes later, without quite knowing how it had all come about, Abby found herself seated with Nick in an out-of-the-way café that was noted for its crêpes, omelets, and French pastries. They had arrived shortly before noon, but now that it was a few minutes past the hour, the rush was on. All the tables were filled and patrons were standing in lines, waiting to be seated.

The Boulangerie advertised itself as "intimate," which was a euphemism for cramped. It contained a dozen tables at most, but a counter for the sale of bakery goods took up a sizeable portion of the floor space, so even that number was a tight fit in such a small room.

It a half-hearted attempt to evoke atmosphere, someone had supplied each table with a faded silk rose in a plastic bud vase, so it certainly wasn't the decor that accounted for the popularity of the café. It was, without a doubt, the excellence of the food that attracted the lunchtime crowds.

Despite the lines, the waitress's movements were unhurried as she set steaming ramekins of onion soup before Abby and Nick and placed a covered basket of croissants on the table. From long experience, she knew that the enticing aromas wafting from the kitchen would dissuade anyone from leaving before they'd been served.

Until the soup was gone, except to request a roll or to ask for the butter, neither Nick nor Abby spoke. It was not until the waitress had removed their empty bowls, preparing to serve their omelets, that Abby remarked, "I thought only local people knew about this place. How did you happen to hear about it?"

"Jamie recommended it," said Nick. "In fact, he gave it rave reviews. He told me the two of you come here occasionally for Sunday brunch."

Abby nodded. "It's very kind of you to take such an interest in Jamie. He's usually such a sobersides, but since you've been coaching him, I hardly recognize him. He's positive he'll make the starting lineup of his Little League team, thanks to you."

"It's my pleasure," Nick replied, shrugging off her gratitude. "I enjoy working with youngsters, and I honestly think Jamie has a lot of natural ability. Considering how fast he's growing, he's remarkably well-coordinated. Besides, it's my way of repaying an old debt."

Smiling reminiscently, Nick went on. "When I was Jamie's age, I was about as clumsy as a boy can be, but I was fortunate enough to have had some instruction from a neighbor who'd played in the minors. Old Clint was quite a character. He never made it past double A ball, but he loved the game and he was a really fantastic coach. I've always attributed the biggest part of my success to the time he invested in me, so after I was drafted by the Tigers, I looked him up to ask if there was anything I could do to repay him, and he said, 'Pass it on.'"

"He sounds very much like Miss Van Zandt, my first piano teacher."

"Did you ever give lessons?" asked Nick. "Aside from the ones you gave Jamie?"

"For a time after our mother died, I did. I got paid for teaching and it helped to stretch our income, but I was never lucky enough to have a student with both talent and interest."

Nick chuckled. "That's one advantage of baseball over music. It's not necessary to acquire a taste for it."

Since baseball was one thing Abby knew she would never acquire a taste for, she might easily have argued this point. In her estimation, baseball was like ketchup—a thing that many people seemed to be quite fond of, but one that she, personally, had never cared for. She found it hard to work up much excitement over a lot of grown men

69

swinging a bat at a ball, while music was something she had felt an affinity for from the start. From her very first piano lesson, music had been as great a necessity to her as breathing.

But their food was served just then, and instead of debating Nick's contention, she watched pensively while he sampled his omelet. When the waitress had refilled their coffee cups and left them alone, Abby asked, "Do you ever miss it? Baseball, I mean?"

Arrested by the question, Nick paused with his fork halfway to his mouth. "For a while I did," he said flatly, "but not anymore. Once I'd had a few months to get accustomed to the idea of not being able to play, I was surprised how little I missed being actively involved."

A smile tugged at the corners of his mouth. "Of course, I'm still one of the most avid fans around. Peggy accuses Ben and me of being fanatics about the sport."

"I know Ben is!" Abby enthusiastically agreed. "Peggy says that once spring training gets under way, she might as well be a stick of furniture for all the notice he takes of her."

Nick's eyes shone with humor and his voice was warm with affection for Peggy as he confided, "She's been on my case because I had a radio installed in the cab of my tractor so I won't miss the play-by-play of the Tigers' games."

"Your tractor?" Abby repeated incredulously. "Are you a farmer now?"

"Part-time," Nick qualified. "It's funny, but I never much liked the farm when I was a kid, and when I went away to college I planned to kick the mud off my shoes and never go back. I'd had the wide-open spaces up to here." With his forefinger he drew an imaginary line just below the angle of his jaw. "And I thought all I wanted was bright lights and crowds of people.

"I guess farming is in my blood, though, because after

a few years I began to look forward to going back for a visit. Finally I realized that I wanted to settle down in the country when I was finished with baseball. After the accident I had offers to coach, and I tried my hand at sportscasting, but in the end I couldn't wait to get back to the farm."

Abby studied Nick, trying to picture him as a farmer. The other night he had come closer to looking the part, for he'd been wearing faded jeans and a lumberjack shirt, but today he was dressed for the city. His slacks and navy blue blazer were obviously custom-tailored, his manners were impeccable, and he looked very much the swinging sophisticate.

He'd found time to have his hair trimmed too, but a few strands were sunbleached to the paleness of straw, while his skin was tanned to the color of fine leather, so it didn't require a great stretch of the imagination to know that he must spend a lot of time outdoors. He was also lean and supple as a greyhound, and the rocklike hardness of his body and the roughness of the calluses on the palms of his hands were further clues to his occupation.

Watching the sinewy play of muscles in Nick's broad wrists as he buttered a croissant, Abby was drawn once again into comparing him with Gordon.

If Gordon had been faced with a predicament similar to Nick's, he would never have openly acknowledged that he'd been influenced by sentiment. Or if he had, he would have summed up the situation tritely and unemotionally by resorting to one of his endless supply of adages.

He'd have said something like "You can take the boy out of the country, but you can't take the country out of the boy." And the maddening thing about it was that he'd have uttered the cliché as if it were original with him.

When Nick unexpectedly glanced at Abby, he caught her studying him. He smiled and her heart skipped a beat. "Eat your omelet before it gets cold." He instructed her

71

as if she were a child. "And stop looking for the traces of the hick in me."

Her pulse had barely enough time to settle into its normal rhythm before he continued in a backwoods drawl. "Shucks, Abby, even in the boondocks we've heard of etiquette. Way back when I was a little boy at my mama's knee, I learned it's not polite to slurp your soup or fan it with your hat to cool it."

Flustered because her thoughts had been so apparent to him, Abby bent her head over her plate. Her omelet was delicious and for a time she concentrated on it. When she felt more composed, she murmured apologetically, "I guess living in the city is no protection against having parochial ideas about some things."

"Anyone can fall into the trap of thinking in stereotypes," Nick good-naturedly agreed.

"You said you were farming part-time?"

"That's right. My folks had about six hundred acres, but my brother Hank inherited Dad's green thumb, so Dad left most of the acreage to him. I've had a house built on the land Dad left me, and I help out whenever Hank needs an extra hand, but I'm more of a hobby-farmer than a real one."

"Do you do some other kind of work, then?"

Nick nodded. "I'm a cartoonist."

So that was why he could take the time to house-sit for the Baumans! Abby wasn't very familiar with cartoons. She followed only one comic strip, a recently syndicated one that chronicled the adventures of a vagabond cat named Sebastian. She supposed she read this cartoon so faithfully because she found certain truths slightly more palatable when they were sugar-coated with humor. On days when the news was especially bad, "Sebastian" was the only part of the paper she read.

Although he was a disreputable drifter who was loyal to no one, although his short-lived affections could be purchased with a can of his favorite brand of sardines, Sebastian was dignified as only a cat can be. And no matter how dire the circumstances, he could be relied upon to land on his feet.

He was also a satirist, and through the device of his rambling from home to home, at times the comic strip poked fun at some of the fads and fancies that swept the country. Everything from the latest fitness craze to the brightest rock star, from current political shenanigans to the newest religious cult, had been grist for Sebastian's mill.

Mostly, though, the cat himself held center stage. Just last Sunday, for example, the cartoon had shown the blasé Sebastian draped belly-down along the top of a fence, watching three battle-scarred tomcats who were vying for the affections of a luscious lady cat.

At first the other three toms were content to show off and strut their stuff while they waited for the lady cat to make her choice. Finally, egged on by Sebastian, the toms began to fight in earnest, and in the last panel the three were seen as nothing more than a ball of flying fur rolling around in the dust of the alley, while Sebastian was walking away with the lady cat, his tail held arrogantly in the air.

"Stick with me, baby, and I'll show you a good time," Sebastian was telling her. "I'm a lover, not a fighter."

Abby's lips curved into a smile as she recalled this cartoon. Her memory of it was so vivid that she could visualize the signature of the artist who drew it. He signed himself simply Gabe.

She looked at Nick, her eyes widening with comprehension. Her voice was high-pitched with amazement as she asked, "Are you the 'Gabe' who draws 'Sebastian'?"

"Guilty," Nick replied tersely. When Abby continued to stare at him, obviously stunned, he added, "Sebastian has cost me so many friends, I should probably take the

Fifth. People either love him or they hate him. There's no in between."

"Well, I'm a fan!" Abby exclaimed. "I can't tell you how much I enjoy reading him. He's such a loveable rascal, and some of the characters he runs into are really incredible. I just adored Trixie Smart."

"Thanks." Nick smiled almost tenderly. "I was fond of her myself. She came close to being the human counterpart of Sebastian."

"Yes, she did. And that overbearing boss of hers—the gossip columnist—"

"Sid Monger?"

Laughing, Abby nodded. "He was a type!"

"That he was," Nick agreed dryly.

"I loved it when they were filming the movie on location at Mt. Rushmore and Mr. Monger concealed his listening devices in Lincoln's nose"—Abby wrinkled her own pert nose to express her amusement—"and the time he marched in that counter-protest, carrying the placard that read HELP STAMP OUT PRIVACY."

For a few moments Abby laughed unrestrainedly. Then she sobered and her eyes grew wide with wonder. "How ever do you come up with all the ideas for the strip?" she inquired.

"There's really nothing mysterious about it. Sometimes readers send me suggestions, but most of it comes straight from life—from people that I've met, or that my friends have known."

"Even Mr. Monger?"

"*Especially* Monger. In my wildest dreams I could never have invented someone as far out as him."

At her doubtful expression Nick said, "Take a look around you, Abby. The eccentrics of this world aren't as rare as you might think. God love 'em, there are times when they seem to have the more conventional types outnumbered."

Taking Nick's advice literally, Abby began glancing around the café, half expecting to see that they were surrounded by comic-strip figures, but she stopped when she came to the couple at the next table.

She stirred uncomfortably when she noticed that the young man was glaring at Nick. The woman with him, on the other hand, was openly admiring Nick.

Since they'd first come into the café, Abby had been vaguely conscious that the couple was eavesdropping—that the woman was casting languishing glances at Nick while her escort was becoming increasingly agitated—but now the man's rancor was so strong that it was very nearly palpable.

If Abby felt the waves of antagonism that emanated from him, however, his girl friend was evidently too caught up with Nick to detect them, for she chose that moment to lean in Nick's direction and say, "Pardon me, but aren't you Nick Gabriel?"

For a few seconds Nick only looked at the woman. Then he inclined his head in acknowledgement. "Yes, I am."

"Would you mind terribly if I asked you for your autograph?" the woman eagerly inquired.

Before Nick could reply, her escort had lumbered to his feet and crossed the small space between the tables. His voice harsh with loathing, the young man asked the other diners in the café, "What d'ya wanna bet he's too dumb to write his name?"

The woman tugged ineffectually at the young man's arm, urging him to sit down. "Please, Donny," she pleaded. "Keep your voice down."

"I don't give a damn who hears me." He pulled angrily away from the woman. "And I sure as hell don't care if some spaced-out, overrated, over-the-hill jock hears me!" Turning aggressively toward Nick, he snarled, "I'll bet you're a washout at indoor sports too, Gabriel."

Abby heard the shocked gasps from the onlookers, but

she didn't see the approach of the manager and busboys as they rushed to intervene. Until later, she didn't know that the chef had overheard Donny's harangue and, still brandishing a carving knife, had run out of the kitchen to help the others subdue him. Nor did she know that Nick had waved off the assistance of the restaurant personnel.

Her field of vision had narrowed until she saw only the wrathful Donny. But from the changing expressions on that young man's face, she could tell that although Nick made no verbal response to the insults, he must have done something to impress Donny as a formidable opponent.

For what seemed like an eternity but was actually a matter of mere seconds, Donny continued to stand at Nick's elbow, glowering down at him. At last his face, which had been livid, grew ashen. His mouth had been set and hard, but under Nick's unblinking gaze it began to quiver.

His eyes shifted around the room as if searching for support, and when none was forthcoming, his shoulders started to sag. His entire body slouched until he seemed to shrink, and Abby suddenly realized that Donny was not the giant his jealous rage had made him appear. At most he was an inch or so taller than her own five feet three, and he just missed being frail.

His Adam's apple bobbled in his scrawny throat as he choked back what must have been a lump of fear, and a collective sigh of relief broke the electrified silence in the café as Donny backed away from Nick and sank into his chair.

For a moment he sat as if frozen, staring beseechingly at his friend. When he was denied her sympathy, he rose and retreated from the café, gray-faced with disbelief that he had been so ignominiously defeated.

As the door closed behind Donny, the manager hurried to Nick's side. "I'm terribly sorry for the disturbance, sir."

"That makes at least two of us," Nick said smoothly,

"but you're not at fault any more than I am. If you'll have the waitress bring our check, we'll be leaving."

"I won't hear of your paying, sir," the manager protested. "After what's happened, I insist that you consider yourselves guests of The Boulangerie."

With a snap of his fingers, the manager cleared a pathway through those of his staff who remained clustered in a semicircle about the table. Shooing the waitresses, busboys, and kitchen workers before him, he led Nick and Abby to the entrance.

"Please, come again, both of you." Smiling and bowing from the waist, the manager saw them out. He was still bowing and smiling when Nick guided Abby away from the café.

CHAPTER FIVE

The line of cars crept along Monroe Street. The bumper-to-bumper flow appeared to be endless, but Nick waited imperturbably until there was enough of an opening that he could safely ease his pickup into the lane of eastbound traffic. He made no attempt to conceal the fact that he was studying Abby while he waited; neither did he try to hide his concern that she might have been unduly upset by the altercation at the café.

It was obvious that Abby was troubled about something. Her manner was distant, and she hadn't said a word since they'd left The Boulangerie. Her eyes were unnaturally bright, glowing like topazes in the creamy pallor of her heart-shaped face.

As he pulled away from the curb, Nick said evenly, "I'm sorry our lunch ended on such a sour note." When Abby ignored this overture, he faked a shiver and quipped, "Brrr. It's getting mighty damned cold in here," but her only response was to sigh and twist her hands together in her lap.

Now Nick decided that music might be just the thing to melt her frosty silence. He turned on the radio and fiddled with the dials until he'd tuned in an FM broadcast of Strauss waltzes.

As soon as the strains of "The Blue Danube" filled the cab, Abby's tension drained away, leaving her limp with weariness. She rested her head against the seat back and turned to look at Nick's rugged profile, wondering if the fact that she had remembered Sunday's "Sebastian" cartoon only minutes before Nick had been challenged by Donny was some sort of omen.

Having seen the way her mother and father had fought, she definitely was not a proponent of purposeless brawls, but unless one was totally without principles, she knew that there were times when one *had* to fight.

She wasn't sure what kind of reaction she had expected of Nick, but after Donny had implied that Nick used drugs, questioned his ability as an athlete, and cast aspersions on his manhood, she certainly wouldn't have thought he'd confine himself to whistling waltzes. Yet that was precisely what he was doing, accompanied by the London Symphony Orchestra.

His behavior seemed strangely inconsistent; until now she would have said that Nick was a man of strong passions.

As disturbing as his calm was, though, part of her marveled at his coolness in the face of adversity. Within the last few years he had lost his wife, sustained an injury that had cost him his career in baseball and, through what must have been a fluke, he'd run afoul of the law. And if that weren't enough, today he'd been called upon to subdue the potential violence of a complete stranger. Despite this, from all outward signs he hadn't a care in the world.

Was it some macho thing with him to suppress his feelings? she wondered. Was he truly not bothered by the distressing turn of events at The Boulangerie? Had Donny violated none of his principles, or did he have no principles

79

to violate? Perhaps, like the cartoon character he had created, Nick was a lover, not a fighter.

For all that there were so many unanswered questions buzzing around in her mind, it never occurred to Abby to ask herself what possible difference Nick's principles, or the lack of them, could make to her.

"The Blue Danube" came to an end and during the lull between musical selections, she asked in a small voice, "Does that sort of thing happen very often?"

"Do you mean the scene with Donny?"

She nodded jerkily.

"Often enough," Nick said dryly. Seeing Abby's alarmed expression, he added hastily, "Not just to me, though. At one time or another, most of the ballplayers I know have had to put up with similar insults. I guess it goes with the turf if you happen to be an athlete with any standing at all in the public eye."

"But why should it?" Abby spoke more strongly this time. "I mean, it was fairly easy to see that Donny was jealous, but even if his girl friend chose to flirt with you, why did he blame you for it?"

"Damned if I know," Nick replied negligently, as if he hadn't given it much thought. "The guys on the team used to speculate that for some youngsters, taking on a professional athlete might be a rite of manhood. In a way, it's straight out of some of the myths about the Old West. If we can place any credence in the TV westerns, in those days the quickest way for an ambitious young man to establish a reputation for toughness was to call out the local gunslinger."

"That does make sense, in a crazy sort of way."

When Nick glanced at Abby, she smiled at him. His eyes swept over her, and though he'd assessed her very briefly, he declared, "Something is still bothering you."

For a moment she hesitated. Then, against her will, she

blurted out, "It's just that I don't understand how you can take it all so calmly!"

Nick's hands tightened on the steering wheel. "What would you have had me do?" he retorted caustically. "Wipe up the floor with the poor bastard?"

"Naturally not!"

"Well, what then? If you think I'm going to lose any sleep because some young punk who hasn't the sense to pour sand out of a boot doesn't like me, you're sadly mistaken!"

As he finished speaking, Nick turned the wheel and braked the pickup sharply, careening to a stop at the side of the road with a shrill squeal of tires that left the acrid odor of burned rubber hanging in the wintry air.

After turning the key in the ignition, Nick shifted position so that he was facing her, sitting with one arm stretched out along the seat back and the other propped across the steering wheel.

"Why are we stopping here?" she asked.

"Because I want to get this ironed out," he said shortly. "I've never cared much for guessing games, so why don't you tell me in plain English what's eating you?"

Abby stared straight ahead at the tree-lined avenue as she answered. "It's just that I think it would be only human to find Donny's comments offensive."

"Oh, I'm as human as the next guy and I found them offensive, all right. But I handled the situation without resorting to bloodletting. It's over and done with, and I refuse to let it ruin the rest of my day."

When she risked a glance at Nick, his eyes intercepted hers and she was captivated by his Svengali-like intensity that seemed to plumb the depths of her mind and read her most intimate thoughts. She wanted to squirm at this frank invasion of her privacy, but she found she hadn't the will to look away. She returned his gaze, losing herself in

81

the warm blue depths of his eyes, trembling breathlessly at the hypnotic sexuality she saw there.

Suddenly Nick grasped her shoulders and drew her toward him.

"Abby"—his breath fanned her cheek as he said her name—"can't you understand that I didn't feel I needed to prove anything to anyone at the café—not to myself, not to Donny, not even to you."

His grip on her gentled and his hands trailed over the tops of her shoulders and along her neck to cup her face between his palms. He tilted her face toward his, his thumbs lazily tracing the tender outline of her mouth.

Abby closed her eyes, unable to withstand the raw desire she read in his. When she swayed weakly in his direction, his arms went around her. His hands moved hotly over her back as he molded her upper body to his, and only then did she realize that she had been waiting for this moment, praying for it, ever since the last time he'd kissed her.

"I understand," she murmured, but the words were lost, absorbed by his mouth as it settled hungrily over hers.

From the first touch of his lips, she was caught up in a dizzying spiral of delight that seemed to have no beginning and no end. A soft moan of pleasure escaped her as his tongue teased her lips apart to taste and entwine with hers. She moved fractionally nearer to him, wrapping her arms around his neck to increase the contact of his body with hers. Her fingers braided themselves through his hair, surprised by its silkiness, to urge him even closer.

His hands had worked their way under her sweater to stroke her back and shoulders, savoring the fine texture of her ski͏͏ ͏railing ecstasy with his fingertips wherever he to͏͏ ͏͏ ͏but the sheer fabric of her slip prevented the ͏ ͏each of them sought.

͏ ͏esperation, without taking his mouth from

82

hers, Nick circled Abby's waist with his hands. Lifting and half-turning her so that she was angled across his lap, he held her with his arm around her shoulders, his own shoulder cushioning her head.

Her flesh seemed to leap with eager anticipation beneath the tantalizing slowness of his exploration as he slid his free hand inside the sweater. It strayed upward from her stomach and over her rib cage to find her breasts, discovering the soft weight, shaping the fullness, cherishing all of the contours. Through the fragile barrier of her slip, he felt her tremble responsively as he inscribed slow circles around a nipple with his thumb.

She gasped with the sheer pleasure of his caresses, and a long shudder passed through Nick as, groaning with reluctance, he relinquished his possession of her mouth, of her breast. He was as shaken as Abby. Although he'd been acutely aware of her, he hadn't been prepared for the volatile urgency of the sexual attraction between them.

"God," he muttered hoarsely, "I haven't felt like this since I was in high school." He let his head fall back against the seat as he fought for control. "At least we both know what we want now."

He felt the slight movement of Abby's head against his chest as she nodded agreement. Her candor pleased him, and his hold on her tightened until his fingers were digging into her side. Wincing, she removed his hand from her waist. Nick watched, perplexity mingling with delight, as she carried his hand to her lips and covered it with small kisses.

"You don't know your own strength," she murmured, her lips brushing his palm. "You have such big hands."

He slanted a rueful smile at her. "Abby, Abby," he said finally, his voice thick with passion. "You're driving me mad."

She met his eyes guilelessly. "I know, I know!" Lacing

her fingers through his, she pressed his hand to her breast to show him that her heart was racing as fast as his.

Nick stirred uncomfortably, wishing he had the will-power to release her. He was tortured by her nearness and he reveled in it. Her eyes were heavy with passion, but when she returned his smile, his attention was diverted to the sweet enticement of her lips. Tempted beyond endurance, he bent over and kissed her again, quick and hard.

"You're a seductive little witch," he said thickly, "but if I do what I want to do to you here, we're liable to be arrested. Let me take you home."

Abby knew what he was asking. She knew she should move away from him, but he was nibbling so persuasively at the side of her neck that she couldn't bear to call a halt to his lovemaking.

"I'd l-like that," she admitted brokenly, "but I can't."

"Why not?"

"I'm supposed to meet Gordon at my place at two o'clock."

For a moment Nick remained immobile. She could tell he was angry before he raised his head, and the spasmodic leap of a muscle at the side of his jaw, the throbbing vein in his temple, offered confirmation of his anger. When he spoke, however, his voice was deceptively quiet.

"Would you mind running that by me again?" he requested.

"I—I said—"

"Never mind," he cut in brusquely. "I believe I heard you correctly the first time." Shaking his head with disbelief, he thrust her roughly back to the passenger side of the cab. "You still haven't told Gordon you're not going to marry him!" he exclaimed derisively. "Don't you think you owe it to the poor schnook to put him out of his misery?"

Abby gasped at his audacity. "I—I haven't really decided—"

84

"Yes, you have," Nick contradicted her explosively. "You've no intention of marrying Gordon. You know it, and I know it, and it's high time Gordon knew it."

"Who appointed you the arbiter of my decisions?" she retorted stiffly. "If you think your opinion of Gordon is of any importance to me, you're assuming too damned much! You've met him once, and if you think that makes you some kind of authority on him, you're wrong. But if you want to know about Gordon, I'll tell you about him.

"Two years ago, when Jamie broke his collarbone skiing, Gordon drove us to the hospital. And when Jamie's Little League team had its father-son banquet, Gordon went with him. He came to most of Jamie's games too, and he doesn't even *like* baseball. And when Jamie won the 'most improved player' award, Gordon was there, and he was as proud as if he were Jamie's father.

"He's always been there for me too, when I've needed a friend—when I've needed someone to talk to, or someone to laugh with, or a shoulder to cry on. He's given and given and given, and he's never asked for anything in return."

Abby was trembling with the effort of controlling her temper. Her hands had curled into tight little fists and every line of her body conveyed her anger. Her voice was impassioned, but it was subdued. By the time she'd concluded, it was almost wispy.

She hadn't noticed that Nick had started the pickup, but when he turned into the supermarket parking lot, she was relieved to see that they had arrived at their destination. He pulled into the parking space beside her own car and killed the engine before he spoke.

"Have you finished?" he inquired coolly.

She nodded.

"You've made Gordon sound like a prince of a guy, and I'll admit that I know very little about him, but I know enough to disagree with you about one thing. He is asking

85

for something. He's asking for *you*. And I know you, Abby, and I still say *you're not going to marry him*."

The abruptness of Nick's movements matched his speech as he reached in front of her, opened her door, and all but shoved her out of the pickup.

"Tell him," he ordered curtly.

Giving her no chance to reply, Nick opened his own door, stepped out of the cab and, without another word or a backward glance, strode across the parking lot toward the supermarket.

Fuming inwardly, Abby watched Nick until he had disappeared into the shopping mall. She wondered, irately, why he thought he had any right to dictate to her. He had no strings on her even if she had let him kiss her and allowed him to take a few liberties. She blushed as she recalled the liberties she had permitted.

She had never felt quite this way before, never experienced such a confusing jumble of emotions. She was excited by Nick's lovemaking and, at the same time, she was miserable because she'd had to decline his offer to take her home. She had wanted so very badly to accept his invitation. She'd longed to go home with him, for she, too, had wanted privacy. She'd wanted him.

As she climbed behind the wheel of her own car, she acknowledged how much she resented Nick's acting as if he owned her. Yes, damn it! She was angry! In fact, never in all her life had she been so blazingly angry.

A small inner voice added that she was also more than a little frightened by the heat of the passion Nick was capable of igniting within her.

No sooner had Abby made this admission than she began to feel more collected. Her innate honesty forced her to admit that a large measure of her outrage was directed at herself. Nick had made her see how unfair she had been to Gordon, how shabbily she had treated him.

86

The moment Nick had said she wasn't going to marry Gordon, she had recognized that this was the truth.

If she had never met Nick, if she'd never kissed him, never known the magic of his lovemaking, she might have been satisfied with a passionless existence. But she had met Nick, and he had kissed her. How could she marry Gordon when her body yearned for Nick? That she had lacked the courage to say no to Gordon's proposal out of fear that she might lose his friendship was no excuse. She had behaved deplorably.

Setting her chin determinedly, Abby resolved she would change all that this very afternoon.

Now that the course of action she must take was clear, she was impatient to get the meeting with Gordon over with. A glance at the digital clock in front of the savings and loan building told her it was already a little after one thirty. Her grocery shopping would just have to wait.

Without further hesitation she started her car and drove away from the shopping center, but she had traveled less than six blocks when the car stalled.

One moment it had been chugging along like the cantankerous vehicle it was, and the next it was losing speed. She pumped the accelerator, but it had no effect. Finally she depressed the gas pedal all the way to the floor, but the car only coughed and sputtered. At the last second she steered it out of the street and it rolled to a stop by the curb.

Minor though it was, she felt like weeping at this new frustration. There were times when she just couldn't cope with having her plans disrupted, and this was definitely one of them.

She slumped over the wheel with her head in her hands, thinking that right about now she would change places with almost anyone else. Since that wasn't possible, she decided she would like to wail and beat her breast—or, better yet, lie down right in the middle of Sherman Avenue and bang her head against the pavement.

As soon as this notion came into her mind, she giggled. She could imagine Jamie's reaction or Gordon's or Nick's if they chanced to come along and see her doing such an outrageous thing.

She yanked on the knob that released the hood latch with more than necessary force, and it came off in her hand.

"What I would really like," she muttered, "is a good, stiff drink."

She clenched her fingers around the knob, wondering whether it might not be wiser to try to find a phone. Perhaps she could still get a message to Gordon before he left the campus.

After a moment's consideration, she discarded this idea. If Gordon was already on his way to meet her, her best hope was to stay with the car. Unless he went miles out of his way, this was the route he would take from the university to her house.

Abby had replaced the knob, lifted the hood, and was looking at the engine as if she could make sense out of the mass of metal and hoses and coils when Gordon's familiar green and white Chevy came into view. For a time it seemed that she'd made the right choice, but her spirits plummeted when he passed her by without so much as slowing down. Though she didn't know how he could have missed spotting her car parked all by itself at the side of the road, it was obvious he hadn't seen her.

She slammed the hood down and kicked the front tire so hard she hurt her toes.

She was locking the passenger door, preparing to leave the car and begin looking for a phone, when Nick's pickup appeared. Thinking she'd weigh the odds a little more in her favor by flagging him down, she started limping as fast as her sore foot would permit along the side of the car toward the street. She stopped when she realized she had misjudged the speed with which he was approaching. It was hopeless. The only option left was to accept the fact that she would have to find a telephone.

She watched resignedly as the pickup sped by. Then, at the last second, Nick's head snapped around in a double take. As incredible as it seemed, he'd seen her!

The pickup swerved into the left-turn lane and the brake lights flashed on as it skidded to a stop at the inter-section with the next cross street. When the light turned green, Nick made a U-turn, circling back in her direction. She followed his progress gratefully as he made another U-turn a block behind her and approached her car for the second time.

Nick pulled in just in front of Abby, left the pickup, and strolled toward her. Her gratitude evaporated when she saw the patronizing expression on his face. He leaned against the front of the car and raised one eyebrow inquir-ingly.

"What's the problem?" he asked.

She bit her tongue, choking back the hot rush of words she wanted to shout at him, and instead described what had happened with the car. When she had concluded, Nick ventured thoughtfully, "Sounds like a frozen fuel line."

Almost groaning aloud that this explanation had not occurred to her, Abby nodded coolly.

"Don't you add antifreeze when you fill the gas tank?" asked Nick.

"In the winter I do, but it's April—"

"It's also right around the freezing mark, which is when you're most apt to have problems with a clogged line."

"Do you think I don't know that?" Abby glared at him. Her fingers itched to slap the self-satisfied smile off his face. "So I forgot to add the blasted antifreeze! Is that a crime? If it is, then abandon me to my fate or something, but please, *please* don't lecture me!"

Nick's eyebrows came together in a puzzled frown. "Why are you whispering?" he asked.

Incapable of replying, Abby turned away from him and stared stonily at the snowbank on the far side of the avenue. When it became apparent that she was not going to answer him, Nick backed away from the car.

"Try it again," he suggested laconically. "It should start now, and if it does, I'll follow you home to make sure you arrive safely."

CHAPTER SIX

Ginger Fiore hadn't been given her nickname because of her hair color. As she was fond of telling new acquaintances, she'd been christened Antoinette LaPlante, and until she'd met her husband, everyone had called her Toni. Although she'd had coal-black hair at the time, Anthony Fiore had begun calling her Ginger on their first date. He'd asked her to be his girl and argued that two Tonys was one too many. Antoinette, he claimed, was too much of a mouthful, while Ginger was better suited to her fiery disposition and the salty language she used.

Whatever the reason, perhaps to show him how willing she was for him to change both her first and last names, she had begun coloring her hair to match his nickname for her.

Whenever Tony heard his wife tell this story, he would laugh and provide the punch line. "And that, folks," he would say, "is the one and only time in the thirty-odd years we've been married that Ginger ever went along with anything I suggested without putting up a damned good fight."

Because it revived memories of the way her parents had

fought, the Fiores' constant wrangling had troubled Abby when she'd first gone to work at The Magic Lantern. Only gradually had she come to see that there was little resemblance between Tony and Ginger's good-natured bickering and the running battles in which her parents had engaged.

After Abby had been in their employ for about six months, Ginger herself explained some of the subtleties of her relationship with her husband.

"Tony knows I love a good argument, so he indulges me, and I heartily endorse the arrangement. Fighting is better for your health than jogging. There's nothing like a good clean fight to purify the air and get the blood pumping. It puts a spring in your step, a sparkle in your eyes, and roses in your cheeks, and the frosting on the cake is that it's so damned much fun making up!" Winking conspiratorially, Ginger added, "That part is the best exercise of all!"

Abby had laughed because she'd known Ginger expected it of her, but privately she'd wondered if there wasn't more fiction than truth to the Fiores' unorthodox method of keeping the zing in their marriage.

That conversation with Ginger had taken place more than three years ago. In the interim Abby had come to know her employers much better, but she still wasn't sure to what extent Ginger had been joking when she'd presented her theory about fighting being good for the health. Since both Ginger and Tony were attractive, vital people with more energy than some who were half their ages, it was possible she'd been dead serious.

It was always difficult to tell whether Ginger was joking. Abby had seen her make light of things she held most dear and remain completely deadpan when she was at her most outrageous.

Tony was the one person who could interpret Ginger's motives with one hundred percent accuracy. "It's a cinch to understand my wife when you know one important fact about her," he'd told Abby. "Ginger is superstitious with a capital *S*. Not about things like spilling salt or hats on the bed or any of the run-of-the-mill phobias some folks have. Her problem is that she's afraid to let on how much she values certain things—yours truly included, of course —for fear she'll offend the gods and they'll retaliate by taking what she prizes away from her."

Tony's insight was not limited to his wife. He found Abby equally transparent. Like Jamie, he had learned to decipher her moods from the way she played piano. On the Wednesday evening following her meeting with Gordon, for instance, Tony knew from the moment she started to play that something was bothering her.

She looked as heartbreakingly lovely as she usually did, and about as unattainable as a moonbeam, in her silvery sheath dress that clung to every curve and hollow of her slender yet full-breasted figure. The crystal-embroidered collar of the dress fastened high around her throat in front, but the neckline plunged almost to her waist in back. Her working wardrobe consisted of several such gowns, all of which were cleverly designed to create the illusion that they were revealing more of Abby than they actually did.

But the funny thing about it was that Abby seemed to don a different personality with the dresses and the more glamorous makeup she applied for her evenings at The Magic Lantern. She purposely cultivated the image of being a self-contained young woman who was quick on the uptake and never at a loss for words—in short, a woman who knew the score. To most of the customers she came across as being a trifle remote. Only with a few of the regulars did she let down her guard.

Tony was accustomed to the change that came over Abby when she was performing. He even had a name for this transformation, calling her alter ego her stage personality, and chiding her gently about it. "Will the real Abby please stand up?" he'd tease.

In return, Abby would laugh. She made no attempt to deny the fact that she was playing a role when she worked. She approached her duties at The Magic Lantern not unlike an actress preparing to go onstage. This made it easier to overcome her natural reticence and to keep the wolves at a distance. It enabled her to fend off passes from would-be Lotharios and amorous drunks, and to deal with their jealous wives without really being touched by any of them.

Unless she was playing something a customer had requested, she tried to keep her selections pleasantly unobtrusive by resorting to medleys of tunes that were in keeping with the tastes of her audience. On special occasions they spotlighted her performance, and only then did she pull out all the stops.

As Ginger had observed, "Abby can play 'Melancholy Baby' and make a grown man weep." This was no exaggeration. One night she'd played "The Way We Were," and by the time she'd reached the coda, there wasn't a dry eye in the house.

Tonight, since most of the crowd was sedate and middle-aged, she was sticking with romantic ballads, but she was playing mechanically, without even a hint of the brilliance that usually shone through.

Her afternoon with Gordon had left a bitter taste in her mouth. She had handled the situation with appalling awkwardness. Instead of making her position clear, she had told him in an ambiguous way that she wasn't going to marry him, leaving the impression that the subject was still open for debate. In spite of her efforts not to offend Gordon, she had wound up by hurting him deeply.

"I know I'm not the most exciting man in the world," Gordon had said as they'd stood uneasily in the living room of the cottage. "I'm well aware that I'm too bookish and that there are times when I tend to be a bit of a prude. I even know that sometimes I can be boring. But I love you, Abby, and I'd be so good to you."

"Oh, Gordon, I know you would," she replied, her voice husky with emotion. "You *have* been good to me. And you're a fine man. You'll make some lucky woman a marvelous husband. But can't you see that I'm not the right woman for you?"

"How can you not be right for me when I want you so much?" Gordon's eyes narrowed accusingly as they roved over her face. "You're doing this because of Gabriel, aren't you?"

Although Nick was only indirectly responsible for her decision, Abby was left speechless by this inspired guess.

"If it's a physical type you want, I'll be happy to demonstrate that I can be just as big a stud as Gabriel."

Gordon started walking toward her, but for every step he took, Abby took one of her own, backing away from him. There was something faintly ominous about him that she found disturbing, but she wasn't truly frightened. He continued stalking her, but even when the arm of the sofa nudged the backs of her knees, causing her to lose her balance, she wasn't afraid of him.

While she was trying to regain her footing, Gordon took advantage of her distraction. All at once he seemed to pounce, closing the distance between them with two long strides, grabbing her and toppling both of them onto the sofa so that she was lying under him.

Even though he was quite thin, he was terribly heavy. She tried to escape the suffocating weight of his body, but he was so much larger that her struggles were as nothing to him as he clamped her head between the iron grip of his hands and ground a brutal kiss onto her lips.

When at last he freed her mouth, she was light-headed with the need for oxygen.

"G-Gordon," she gasped. "What are you doing? You're hurting me!"

"Damn you, Abby! Do you think you haven't hurt me?"

Despite his harsh words, he braced himself on his elbows, relieving her of the burden of most of his weight. Drawing in a deep draft of air, she protested, "Th-this isn't like you!"

"How would you know?" he sneered. "You with your touch-me-not ways. Well, I see through you now. I see that you're nothing but a nasty little tease. I see that your precious innocence is all an act. But you know nothing about me."

Gordon's clean-cut features were marred by the petulant droop of his mouth. For a moment he looked so much like a sulky little boy that Abby had an insane impulse to laugh. Then his gaze wandered over her, lingering on the hectic rise and fall of her breasts as she labored to fill her lungs. The calculating glitter in his eyes made him seem a stranger, and she knew that he was impervious to reason. When his mouth swooped toward hers, she renewed her struggles.

She fought in earnest now, turning her head from side to side to avoid his questing mouth, trying to hit and scratch him, wanting only to be free of the hands that were tearing at her clothing in their frenzy to find and explore her body. This was not the same Gordon she had known all these years, and she no longer cared whether she hurt him.

After a brief, uneven contest, he managed to capture both her wrists in one hand and draw them cruelly over her head. Her feet were still unconfined and she tried to kick him, but he anticipated her every move and quelled it with ease. He laughed coldly at her efforts, as though her puny resistance only added to his enjoyment. Finally, growing impatient with her weakening attempts to evade him, he closed one hand tightly over her throat.

"Don't fight me," he threatened, panting a bit from the exertion of restraining her. "I don't want to hurt you, but I will if I have to. I swear I will."

White-faced with pain and terror, Abby saw him through the haze of tears that had welled into her eyes. "Please—" Her lips moved to plead with him, but she was unable to force the smallest sound past his constricting grip on her neck.

"Please—" She tried again, and again succeeded only in mouthing the word.

Evidently this was enough to reach him, however, for his hold on her slackened.

"Please," she repeated, and this time managed to whisper the plea.

Gordon shook his head, but not in denial. It was as if he were trying to think clearly.

"I'm sorry I've hurt you, Gordon, but I truly never meant to. Please let me go."

At the slight vibration of her voice against his fingers, he studied the hand that was still loosely wrapped about her throat, his expression changing rapidly, from surprise to bewilderment to horror.

"My God!" he cried hoarsely.

Releasing her, he rolled to his feet and staggered away from the sofa to stand stiffly on the far side of the room.

Abby eased to a sitting position and swung her feet to the floor, closing her eyes against the dizziness that assailed her. When she was a little steadier, she began to rub her wrists, attempting to restore the circulation to them. She felt numb all over and she was only vaguely conscious of Gordon's continued presence until she heard him cry her name.

Between the sobs that wracked him, he cried that he was sorry, that he didn't know what had come over him, and her fear was banished by the despair she heard in his voice.

She went to him, took him in her arms, and held him until the awful remorse had passed, weeping a little herself as she comforted him. And for that small span of time, she came very close to loving Gordon—not in a romantic way, not as a lover, but with an affection that was almost maternal.

"It's all right, Gordon," she had murmured over and over again. "It was my fault as much as yours."

They had parted with the promise to see each other soon, but both of them knew that, barring the unforeseen, they would not meet again.

That night, for the first time that she could recall, Abby found no solace in her music. Perhaps she might have if she'd been able to play something somber, but it was impossible to submerge her memories of the afternoon in the light show tunes she played in the lounge.

She had been sincere in accepting that part of the guilt for Gordon's near-assault was hers. She had to admit that while she hadn't intentionally acted the tease with him, she had led him on, and in the hours since they'd said good-bye, her mind had rerun the scene with him countless times. But it was only as she sat at the piano in The Magic Lantern that the things she might have said to salve Gordon's wounded pride occurred to her. As the evening waned, in the quiet time preceding the rush of theatergoers coming in for a late supper, she chastised herself for not remembering to wish Gordon well in his new job at Dryden University.

"How about trying a few choruses of 'St. Louis Blues'?"

Jarred from her musings by Ginger's smoky voice, Abby looked up to see her leaning against the piano. Her smile invited an exchange of confidences, and the song she'd mentioned was more in keeping with Abby's frame of mind, but it also reminded her of Nick. Abby was swamped by a wave of longing for him—the need to see

98

him, to be with him, to touch him, was so overwhelming that it was very nearly unbearable.

"On second thought"—Ginger hastily revised her suggestion—"how about taking a break?"

Without waiting for Abby to respond, Ginger led the way toward an isolated booth in the darkest corner at the back of the lounge, pausing only to signal Merle Halloran as they passed the bar. Within seconds after they had seated themselves, the cocktail waitress appeared with a coffee for both of them.

"Thanks, Merle," said Ginger. Smiling, Merle departed and Ginger remarked lightly, "Maybe I should have ordered something stronger for you."

"No," Abby replied. "This is fine."

Ginger frowned worriedly. "There's nothing wrong with Jamie—"

"No. Jamie's fine, just fine."

"Okay, I'll buy that." Ginger laughed a little with relief. "The coffee's fine, and Jamie's fine, but you're not. If you don't mind my saying so, you look like you've just lost your last friend."

"Not my last one, but I've lost one of the best." Abby smiled wanly. "Gordon and I had a terrible row this afternoon."

"He'll come around," Ginger declared airily. He would, she thought. He was like the proverbial bad penny, and that kind always did.

"Not this time. He'll be leaving for the West Coast at the end of the semester, and I won't be going with him."

Ginger's finely tweezed eyebrows climbed until they had disappeared beneath the bright fringe of curls on her forehead. "Do you mean you finally got around to turning down his proposal?"

Abby nodded. "Very clumsily, I'm afraid."

She looked so miserable that Ginger extended herself to make some soothing comments about how a clean break was less painful in the long run, and how it was better that Abby and Gordon had discovered they weren't suited to each other before they were married.

Judging from Abby's downhearted expression, Ginger knew that her little pep talk hadn't done much good, but at least she could report to Tony that she'd found out what was troubling Abby and that she'd done her best to cheer her up. It was at his instigation that she'd approached Abby.

Tony and his damned clairvoyance, thought Ginger without rancor. It hadn't been easy to offer sympathy to Abby because of her break-up with Gordon when secretly she was pleased about it.

In her opinion Gordon Sprague was a fool. He'd offended dear Harlan Crowley by telling him, point-blank, that he was a tightwad. He'd said that anyone who could afford to dress as well as Mr. Crowley did shouldn't hesitate over replacing his ill-fitting dentures.

Not only that, he'd had the unmitigated nerve to look down his aristocratic nose at Tony and her. And to add insult to injury, although The Magic Lantern was one of the finest restaurants in Madison, he'd made it plain that he frowned on Abby's "wasting" her talents by working for them.

Ginger knew very well how gifted Abby was, and she might have conceded that Gordon had a point if he hadn't been so outspoken about the fact that he considered The Magic Lantern too "crass," too "lowbrow," to provide a proper showcase for such an accomplished pianist.

But even if Gordon had been more congenial the few times they'd met, even if he'd been the nicest man in the world, Ginger would have had serious reservations about whether he and Abby could ever have been happy together.

Ginger believed that Abby was more of a sensualist than she realized and that it would take a lustier type than

Gordon Sprague to keep her content. She needed a man who would treat her like a woman instead of using her as a sounding board for his theories. She needed a man who could waken her instincts and fire her senses and get her hormones flowing. A man, for instance, like the one who had just come into the lounge.

She watched the tall, tawny-haired man who was standing at the far end of the bar speaking to Carl Lykins, one of the bartenders. She admired the perfect proportions of his lean body and visualized the sinuous rippling of muscles beneath his navy blue blazer. She liked the way he smiled, open and warm, as he leaned across the bar to shake hands with Carl, and she could imagine the firm self-assurance of his handshake.

Now there, she told herself with silent vehemence, *is a man!*

Because of the darkness at the corner table, Ginger's scrutiny of him went unnoticed as he talked with Carl. It became apparent that he was questioning the bartender about something—or someone. At one point both men glanced toward the piano and Carl shook his head. Was the stranger inquiring about Abby?

Dragging her eyes away from the man, Ginger looked curiously at Abby, but she found no answer to her question in the way Abby sat hunched over the table, staring into her coffee. Since her back was to the man, it was obvious she hadn't seen him.

Ginger looked back at the stranger in time to see him turn away from Carl and walk toward the dining room. He moved with lithe, easy confidence, an athletic swing to his wide shoulders and narrow hips.

It was not until he was out of sight that Ginger realized she had been holding her breath. Exhaling in a sigh, she told herself again, *Now there is a man!*

She'd bet her life that he knew everything worth knowing about how to make a woman feel like a woman. She would even bet he had hair on his chest!

With another small sigh Ginger's wandering attentions returned to Abby. When she saw that that young woman was still lost in contemplation, Ginger smiled cryptically and shook her head, mocking herself for being so fanciful.

Tony thought women never speculated about men. He could divine her thoughts about most things, but after more than thirty years of marriage, he still believed that only men had fantasies about the opposite sex. Bless the man! Ginger thought wryly. If he ever learned the truth, it would probably blow his mind!

"Well, I'll be!"

Abby looked up when she heard Ginger's softly voiced exclamation. Turning her head to follow the direction of the older woman's gaze, she saw Tony threading his way through the lounge toward their table. All the warmth and light from the candle that flickered on the table seemed to gather in her eyes when she saw that Nick was close behind him.

She watched their progress, not quite believing that she wasn't imagining things. She had wanted to see Nick so badly that her need had become a hollow ache inside her. Now he was here, smiling at Ginger as Tony introduced them, smiling at her in a protective, possessive way, so that her cheeks bloomed with the rosy tide of color that flooded them.

"Nick Gabriel." Ginger repeated his name thoughtfully as they shook hands and, for a moment, Abby worried that she was going to comment on the narcotics charges against Nick. But she didn't. Abby didn't know whether Ginger knew about the indictment, but she only inquired, "Say, didn't you used to be a baseball player?"

"That's right, Ginger," Tony interjected before Nick could reply. "Except that Nick wasn't just another player. He was one of the greatest pitchers going!"

"Well, well," said Ginger, flashing her most ingratiating smile at Nick. "I thought when you came in that I'd seen you somewhere before. I never forget a face, do I, Tony?"

Her husband nodded, confirming her claim.

"Tell me, Nick," she asked, "what brings you to The Magic Lantern?"

"Abby," Nick answered smoothly. "Her car stalled this afternoon, and since I happened to be at the Civic Center tonight, I thought I'd stop in to make sure her car wasn't giving her any more trouble."

While Ginger was wondering why Abby had never mentioned that Nick Gabriel was a friend, and was trying to think of a diplomatic way to find out how far their friendship had advanced, Tony changed the subject.

"Is this production of *Carmen* as good as I've heard it is?" he asked, naming the opera that was currently playing at the Civic Center.

Abby didn't hear Nick's reply, nor could she concentrate on the exchange of pleasantries that ensued. The set of Nick's broad shoulders was relaxed and easy as he sat with one arm stretched along the back of the bench behind her, and if she were to lean back just a touch she would necessarily find herself within his casual embrace. She was tingling with the awareness of this possibility and from the pressure of his thigh against her own, and she found it impossible to think of anything but him.

He glanced down at her, half smiling, and though she tried to tear her gaze away from his, she couldn't until she'd seen the reflection of her own naked longing in the fathomless blue depths of Nick's eyes.

She replaced her coffee cup in its saucer with a clatter. Her hands were shaking with the intensity of her reaction to him and she folded them tightly in her lap to conceal them.

Suddenly she was so befuddled that it was not until

Ginger and Tony were making their farewells that she was able to make any sense of the conversation.

"We hope we'll see you again during your stay." Tony's smile reinforced the sincerity of his remark.

"In fact, we insist!" Ginger seconded her husband's sentiment. "You really must come for dinner some evening—as our guest, of course."

Puzzled because the usually unflappable Ginger was practically gushing, Abby said uncertainly, "I suppose I'd better be getting back to work too."

"Take your time, dear," Ginger hurriedly instructed. "Come to think of it, since it's almost midnight, why don't you go on home."

"Good idea, Ginger," Tony enthused. "That way she won't have to keep Nick waiting."

While Abby stared dumbly at Ginger and Tony, wondering if they had taken leave of their senses, Nick replied steadily, "Oh, but I don't mind waiting. Listening to Abby play piano is certainly no hardship."

"Well, all right," Ginger conceded. Then, wagging her finger at Abby, she cautioned, "But just for a few minutes."

The Fiores rose to leave the table and Nick got to his feet, but Abby remained seated until Ginger and Tony had returned to the dining room. As she slid out of the booth, she said, "It was kind of you to come by, but you really needn't stay. My car was running perfectly well when I drove to work, and it's warmer now than it was earlier today."

"Actually your car is only part of the reason I'm here." Nick guided her toward the front of the lounge with a proprietary hand on the bare skin of her back. "I saw Jamie earlier tonight, and from what he told me, I thought you might like someone to talk to." He felt the slight hesitation in Abby's step and added gruffly, "Or a shoulder to cry on."

104

At the instant Nick said the words, Abby realized that there was nothing she would like better than to throw herself into his arms and cry out her sorrow on his shoulder. But this was neither the time nor the place for tears.

She tried to keep her face averted as she took her seat at the piano, but Nick forced her to look at him, turning her face toward his with one hand gently framing her cheek. He saw the tears that had filled her eyes and dropped down to sit beside her on the piano bench.

"Was it that bad?" he asked softly.

Blinking rapidly and pressing her lips together to keep from crying, Abby nodded.

Nick's eyes were infinitely blue as he scanned her face. In spite of the darkness of the lounge, in spite of her attempts to cover it with makeup, he saw what appeared to be a small bruise at the corner of Abby's mouth. Before she could stop him, he touched the spot lightly, testing the silky skin with one fingertip, and she flinched, confirming his suspicions.

"Did Gordon do that?"

"Please, Nick—"

"Did he?" Nick demanded. Although Abby's lips tightened, indicating her refusal to reply, he read the answer in her eyes. His voice was harsh with fury as he muttered, "That bastard!"

"Please, Nick," Abby repeated tremulously. "I can't take your anger just now."

"Not even if it's in your behalf?"

"Not even that."

For long moments he was silent. Then, to her surprise, a smile softened the hard line of his mouth. As if he were thinking out loud, Nick said, "So *that's* why you were whispering!"

His hand moved over her cheek to curve with gentle insistence around the nape of her neck. "Okay, sweetheart, if that's the way you want it, I'll go along with you.

But I don't intend to let you off the hook indefinitely. Sooner or later, I'll expect you to take a lot more from me than anger." Under his breath he concluded, "And I'll expect a hell of a lot more from you."

CHAPTER SEVEN

Abby awoke thinking about Nick and she went to bed thinking about him. His image haunted her during the day and invaded her dreams at night. She tried to concentrate on other things, but she seemed to have lost control of her thoughts.

It didn't help that Jamie talked about him incessantly, and the Fiores raved about him. At home it was "Nick said this," and "Nick did that," and at work she was bombarded with questions about him.

The only time she found any respite from this mental torment was when she was actually with Nick, and that was worse, because when she was with him, she couldn't think at all.

She saw him several times in the next few days. They met for lunch on Thursday and Friday, and on Saturday night he came into The Magic Lantern again. He sat at the bar, listening to her play and talking with Carl Lykins and Harlan Crowley until it was time for her break. Then he led her to the booth in the back corner of the lounge.

For perhaps a quarter of an hour they sat side by side. They talked, but afterward she remembered nothing that either of them had said. She was aware only of Nick's arm around her shoulders and of the way he looked at her, as if he were wondering what it would be like to make love to her.

"Walk me to my truck," Nick requested easily before she returned to the piano. Uncertain of her voice, she nodded.

As they left the restaurant and strolled toward the parking lot, he put his arm around her again, tucking her close to his side. She wanted to keep on walking beside him forever, but all too soon they reached the pickup.

Nick didn't release her though. He seemed to want to go on holding her as much as she wanted him to. He withdrew his arm from her shoulders, but his hand slid slowly down her inner arm, barely grazing the sensitive skin, to link with her hand.

He moved a step away from her and studied her face while she stood indecisively, her heart pounding, shivering a little in the cool night air from the clammy feel of her satin evening gown clinging to her skin.

Her breath caught in her throat when Nick's gaze left her face to travel over her body. It was as though he caressed her, warmed her, with his eyes. His glance returned to her breasts, lingering on their voluptuous fullness until she felt giddy.

It seemed to her that she had been holding her breath for hours when, with his free hand, he began outlining the neckline of her dress, allowing the backs of his fingers to brush across the upper curve of her breasts as he followed the dainty spaghetti straps to the point where they tied at the back of her neck.

She gasped for air. "What in the world do you think you're doing?"

"I'm just waiting to see what happens to that delightfully provocative dress when you exhale. From where I'm standing, it looks as if it would be a spectacular feat of engineering if it stays up on its own when you're not holding your breath."

"Thank you for your concern, but I assure you it's quite securely anchored."

Smiling wickedly into her eyes, he grasped one of the ties as if threatening to tug it free. She endured this submissively although her heart was pounding so loudly that she thought surely Nick must be able to hear it.

"What happens if I undo this little bow?" he inquired, his eyes glinting with devilish intent.

Feeling compelled to do something to break the spell he was casting over her, she slipped into her onstage personality and pretended indifference. "In that case, I can make no guarantees."

Although she felt Nick tense, his hand continued to tease her. "You're different when you're at work."

"Well, you know what they say, 'Variety is the spice,' and all that sort of thing. When I'm good, I'm very, very good, but when I'm bad, I'm terrific."

Nick's hand squeezed hers punishingly. "Can it, Abby," he reproached her curtly. "That's not you."

Her resistance melted. Moistening her lips, she whispered raggedly, "N-no. I know it isn't."

He pulled her close again, wrapping both arms around her and running his hands over the satiny skin of her back, her shoulders, her arms, while his mouth traced the delicate outline of her face.

"You feel as good as you look," he murmured thickly.

She wound her arms around his waist and pressed closer to him, rubbing her cheek against his as her hands crept upward along his back and over his shoulders, delighting in his lean, rugged strength.

"Oh, Nick"—her voice was barely aud͟   do you!"

His arms tightened so convulsively, she t͟   might crack. She clung to him, confuse͟

109

mingling of pleasure and pain she felt as he lifted her completely off her feet. For a time he held her this way, so close it was as if he were trying to meld her body with his. At last he loosened his hold on her, letting her slide down against the proud, hard length of his body until her feet touched the ground.

For a few moments Nick stared down at her.

"Tomorrow is your day off?"

"Y-yes."

"I'll see you then." In the darkness his eyes seemed to smolder, blazing a fiery blue that mirrored her own desires. They burned into her eyes, daring her to refuse.

"Yes," she agreed gravely.

"About two o'clock?"

"Two o'clock," she echoed, her voice shaking with an excitement she could no longer contain.

A terrible feeling of emptiness and loss gripped her when Nick moved away from her to climb into the pickup. And the instant he drove away, she was so lonely for him, she thought she couldn't bear waiting until the next afternoon to see him again.

It was sometime later before she began to question the wisdom of seeing him the next day.

The following morning was the kind that made Abby feel glad to be alive. After almost a week of temperatures in the fifties, most of the snow had melted and ice floes sailed through patches of open water on Lake Mendota. The air was balmy and golden with sunshine, lush with birdsong, redolent with the richly invigorating odor of the awakening earth.

Suddenly it was spring, and to celebrate the season, when she and Jamie got home from Palm Sunday services that morning, Abby threw open all the doors and windows the cottage. After the winter-long necessity of storm windows and artificially heated rooms, she reveled in the ritual.

From the way Jamie was sprawled on the sofa with the Sunday edition of the *State Journal* strewn around him, it was apparent that he was immune to the seductions of nature, but Abby wasn't. She felt restless and full of energy, too energetic to sit still.

After changing into faded jeans and an oversized T-shirt, she tied her hair back with a piece of yarn to keep it out of her eyes while she tackled some serious cleaning projects.

Unlike her, Jamie read the whole newspaper, from the front page to the classifieds, and since he appeared to be settled in the living room for the duration of the morning, she decided to begin with the kitchen. It seemed the perfect opportunity to launder curtains and wash windows and sort out cupboards.

Soon she was up to her elbows in hot, soapy water, handwashing her mother's collection of majolica and humming as she worked. Now and again she stopped to admire the varied shades of green, the lovely designs and graceful shapes of her favorite pieces of the pottery.

Abby's grandmother, Thea Douglas, had started the collection with several plates which were purchased when she and her husband had visited Italy on their honeymoon. Audrey had told Abby the history of each of the souvenirs and Abby loved the oldest pieces best of all. She barely remembered her grandmother, but her few memories of Thea were exceedingly pleasant ones.

Abby often regretted that Jamie had never had the chance to know the silver-haired lady with the soft southern drawl. Thea had always smelled of violets, and that fragrance still reminded Abby of her grandmother. In old age Granny Douglas had suffered greatly from arthritis, cataracts had left her nearly blind, and her fine pink-and-white complexion had been so crisscrossed with lines that

111

it resembled crumpled tissue paper, but she had kept her gracious manner until the day she died.

Knowing how much Audrey treasured the majolica, Bruce Riordan had brought additions for the collection whenever he'd returned from his travels. More often than not, he'd given them to Audrey as peace-offerings, and for a while after she'd received his latest gift, Audrey had been sweetly compliant and affectionate and marital bliss had reigned.

It had never lasted, though. Eventually the novelty had worn off and she had become strident again. She would resume her prodding and nagging, Bruce would counter with one of his tirades, and all the old disputes would be revived.

Still, even the pieces of majolica her father had added to the collection were associated with the rare, tranquil periods her parents had enjoyed, and Abby handled the pottery lovingly as she washed it and replaced it on its shelves in the breakfront.

The phone rang once or twice, but she left it to Jamie to answer. Most of their incoming calls were for him. He might not like talking on the phone quite as much as he liked baseball, but it was a close second.

As the morning wore on, Jamie wandered into the kitchen a few times to look for a snack or to exclaim over something he'd read in the paper. He happened to come in while she was rehanging the curtains and she enlisted his aid, but even as he steadied their rather rickety stepladder, he continued reading. Never once did he see how cheerful the kitchen looked with the sun sparkling on the windowpanes and the crisply laundered curtains billowing in the playful breezes.

His lack of interest was so marked that Abby's enthusiasm flagged, but only temporarily. She knew that Jamie would certainly comment on the fact if he had no clean clothes to wear, or if—perish the thought!—his

112

meals weren't ready on time. But aside from matters that affected his physical comfort, he never seemed to notice her efforts as a homemaker, much less appreciate them.

As she gathered supplies to start cleaning the living room, Abby philosophically told herself that no matter how you cut it, housework was a thankless task. But at least she had the satisfaction of knowing the windows were washed and the majolica polished, and she wouldn't have to do those particular chores tomorrow.

Jamie was deep in the comics when Abby came into the living room, pushing the vacuum cleaner in front of her. She had plugged the cleaner in and was about to turn it on when her brother burst out laughing.

"Have you read 'Sebastian' today?" he asked, still snickering. "He's in his usual spot on the fence in back of the apartment building, but there's some guy inside the ground floor unit who's singing 'Asleep in the Deep' at the top of his lungs, and he's keeping Sebastian awake. So he goes on down the fence—"

Jamie continued speaking, but he could have been talking gibberish for all Abby knew. Although she gave the impression that she was attentive, she had stopped listening to him. When Jamie finished his narration of the cartoon and looked at her expectantly, she forced a smile, but as strained as her display of amusement was, it was enough to satisfy her brother. Jamie was still laughing as he laid the comics aside and unfolded the sports page.

"He got him right between the *be* and the *ware*," said Jamie. "Isn't that something?" In the next instant, the teen-ager was absorbed in reports about spring training.

It was not as easy for Abby to turn her thoughts away from Nick. Jamie's mentioning "Sebastian" had brought her questions about him sharply into focus, and her pleasure in the springlike day was dulled. In a die-hard effort to rekindle her interest in the homely chores at hand, she flipped the switch on the vacuum cleaner and the motor roared to life. She propelled the cleaner about the room, making increasingly smaller circles around Jamie, but she did it automatically, thinking about Nick while she worked.

Her mind shuttled back and forth like a mouse caught in a maze, trying to unravel the enigma Nick Gabriel presented. And with every blind alley she explored, she felt more hopelessly trapped.

When they had occurred to her last night, her doubts had kept her from sleeping. She had told herself that she was playing with fire if she didn't keep her distance from Nick. Their mutual attraction was elemental and, at least for her, could prove to be dangerous. Every time she saw him she became more convinced of this and less capable of resisting his magnetic appeal. It was ironic in a way. She had dreamed of being swept off her feet, but now that Nick could make her dream become a reality, she was frightened because he might.

Confronted by passions that were totally new to her, she was unsure of herself, but she was even more unsure of Nick. What was more, she didn't know whether she liked the tempestuous effect he had on her. How could she when she knew so little about him?

It was perplexing that he should have remained so carefree in the face of his misfortunes. Didn't this indicate a certain callousness, a shallowness of feeling? And to her, both of his chosen professions seemed rather frivolous; baseball in particular was a child's game.

Come to think of it, maybe Nick was like the cartoon character he had created. Maybe, like Sebastian, he was a hedonistic rogue who valued only the absurdities of life. Maybe, like Sebastian, he was faithful to no one but himself, cared for no one but himself. Maybe Nick just didn't give a damn.

She knew the Baumans were fond of him, but he'd been married to their daughter, so it wouldn't be unnatural if

114

Ben and Peggy were biased in his favor. She knew he was kind to Jamie, but she half-suspected that his motives were not entirely unselfish. After all, hero worship could be balm for an inflated ego.

The only thing she was certain about so far as Nick was concerned was that all he had to do was touch her and she went up in flames. And the effect he had over her was fast becoming habit-forming.

There were times when she wished she'd never met him. Before he had come into her life, everything had been so much simpler. She'd had her brother and her work and her friends. She'd had Gordon's friendship.

In the two short weeks since Nick had come on the scene, the peaceful order of her world had been disrupted. Gordon had become a stranger, and with each day that passed she was becoming more of a stranger to herself.

While Abby was grappling with her questions about Nick, her circling maneuvers with the vacuum cleaner had brought her closer to Jamie. Now, as he lifted his feet out of the way so she could clean the carpeting in front of the sofa, he grimaced, making no secret of how disgruntled he was at the disturbance.

"Boy, oh, boy," he grumbled when she had finished and switched the cleaner off. "You sure are having an attack of the neats."

Abby glanced derisively at a pair of his sneakers that were poking out from their hiding place beneath the sofa, at the pages of the *State Journal* that were scattered about, at his sweater hanging over the doorknob, at a glove abandoned by the windows and its mate on the piano bench, and at his book bag and Windbreaker that had been left on a chair.

"Don't worry," she retorted tartly. "It doesn't appear to be contagious."

It was unlike Abby to lose her patience with him and Jamie stared at her, astonished.

"Okay, okay, I get your drift," he said placatingly, slipping on the shoes and making a great show out of collecting the sections of the paper.

His attempt to smooth her ruffled feelings was so obvious that Abby felt a pang of conscience for having snapped at him. Before she could make amends, however, the telephone rang.

"I'll get it," Jamie cried. "It's probably Shane."

His good intentions forgotten at the prospect of talking to his best friend, he raced to answer the phone, leaving Abby to finish picking up the newspaper. She had actually begun arranging the sections in an orderly stack when irritation overtook her. Tossing the paper disgustedly onto the coffee table, she stalked out of the living room.

To hell with it! she told herself. *It's Jamie's clutter, and he can damned well clear it away.*

As for her, she was going to relax in a leisurely bath and forget about being the responsible older sister, forget her failures as a reliable friend. She was going to forget about Jamie, forget the whole sorry mess with Gordon, but most of all, she was going to try to forget her doubts about Nick.

The bath didn't have quite the calming effect Abby had hoped for, but it helped. Adjusting the taps so a trickle of hot water would keep the water from cooling, she lay back, closed her eyes, and tried to make her mind a blank. For a long time she didn't move.

After half an hour or so, Jamie knocked on the door and called rather tentatively, "Hey, Abby. You asleep in there?"

"No, Jamie, I'm not," she answered without opening her eyes. She only wished she could fall asleep.

"Well, uh—I just wanted to ask if I can spend the night at Shane's house. We thought we'd go down to University Square and take in the matinee of *The Empire Strikes Back.*"

"I thought you'd already seen it—"

"It's the kind of movie you don't get tired of," Jamie interrupted eagerly. "It's all squared with Shane's mom and dad."

"What about your route?"

"Gary Everett said he'd deliver the papers for me tomorrow."

Abby opened her eyes and sat up, peering intently through the steam that wafted from the water as if she might be able to see Jamie in spite of the closed door. Since the next week was Easter vacation, she could think of no reason to object to Jamie's plans. Besides, it would probably be good for both of them to have a break from one another.

"All right, then," she said. "Do you have enough money?"

"Yeah, I have plenty."

"What about lunch?"

"We'll get something downtown." For a few seconds he was silent, but she sensed he was still at the door.

"Is there something else?" she called.

"I put my stuff away."

This roundabout bid for approval brought a smile to her lips. "Thanks, Jamie. I'm sorry I was cross with you."

"That's okay, Sis. I should've done it before," he replied magnanimously. "Say—uh, you wouldn't want to go to the movie with Shane and me, would you?"

Jamie sounded so dutiful and, at the same time, so solicitous, Abby didn't know whether to laugh or to cry. He would hate it if she accepted. He'd find it terribly embarrassing to have his older sister tagging along. She knew how much it had cost her brother to make the offer, and the last of her irritation with him was supplanted by tenderness.

Clearing her throat, Abby exerted herself to reply evenly, "Thanks again, Jamie, but I don't think so. Maybe some other time."

"You're sure?"

"Positive."

"Catch ya tomorrow then," said Jamie, and before Abby could respond, he was gone.

She didn't linger in the tub after she'd heard him leave the house. It was after one o'clock and Nick would be arriving soon. Her conscience was bothering her because she hadn't told Jamie she was seeing Nick today. It made her feel as if she were planning on doing something clandestine when, in fact, she had only good intentions.

She left the bath in a rush when a small inner voice reminded her that the road to hell was paved with those.

It was only when she stood in front of her closet that Abby realized she had no idea of Nick's plans for the afternoon, and consequently no idea how to dress. Still debating what she should wear, she wandered out of her bedroom and along the hallway.

The cottage was strangely neat without the trail of belongings that Jamie dropped, like so many breadcrumbs, to chart the path between the front door and his room.

After the warmth of her bath, since she was wearing only a light dressing gown, she felt quite chilly. She began closing the windows, ending with those nearest the piano.

As if to match her mood, clouds had drifted across the face of the sun, making the day seem dark and cheerless. It was so quiet in the cottage that she started when she absentmindedly reached out to touch the piano keyboard and the note she had struck rang out.

Did middle C sound a trifle flat? She tapped the key again, followed it with a scale, and decided she would have to have the piano tuned before much longer.

Idly, with one finger moving almost caressingly over the keys, she picked out a plaintive melody, stopping abruptly when she recognized she was playing "St. Louis Blues."

118

To drown out the tiniest echo of that evocative tune, with the other hand she jabbed out a rippling arpeggio, loud and deep, and followed that with a bass chord.

The booming resonance of the bass chord was so satisfying that she seated herself on the bench, launching into the Appassionata Sonata even as she did so. She attacked the theme ferociously, as if she were locked with it in mortal combat, emphasizing the tense struggle for dominance between the treble and the bass until the walls of the living room reverberated with a powerful crescendo and she was surrounded by the music, lost in it.

On and on she played, crashing relentlessly through the quieter second movement in her eagerness to expend her fury in the allegro, her chaotic emotions whipping her into a frenzy that brought beads of perspiration to her forehead.

She lost track of time and was unaware that Nick had let himself into the cottage until the final notes of the finale had died away. She was so drained that she reacted as if in slow motion to the sound of applause.

Looking up, she saw Nick standing by the windows, watching her.

"Bravo, Abby! That was brilliant."

His eyes roamed over her, taking in every detail of her dishabille, noticing the faraway light in her eyes that made her look as if the music had transported her to some other world. She was breathing rapidly through slightly parted lips and her hair was damp from exertion. A few tendrils had escaped the yarn and were clinging to her temples in wispy babylike curls. But there was nothing remotely childish about the lush contours of the breasts that were clearly outlined by the thin cotton lawn of her robe.

At the same instant that Nick's eyes returned to her face, Abby realized how nearly transparent the robe was and crossed her arms protectively over her breasts, shielding them from his view. He chuckled, amused by her belated display of modesty, and she flushed hotly.

Her embarrassment seemed to spur him on. He moved closer, lounging against the piano with his arms folded across his chest in a mocking imitation of her posture.

"I must admit, though," he said dryly, "I find Beethoven too belligerent at times. It strikes me as an inauspicious start to our afternoon to hear you playing like that."

She stared at him, surprised he had recognized the composer. "Y-yes. Well, the Appassionata isn't precisely my cup of tea, but today it suited my mood."

"That's what I was afraid of!"

He turned his mouth down at the corners, but his eyes continued to challenge her.

"Do you usually barge into someone's house without knocking?" she responded defensively.

"Oh, but I did knock," Nick countered without missing a beat. "When you didn't answer, I assumed, since you were expecting me, you wouldn't mind my coming in."

Abby scanned the room wildly, trying to think of some means of making a dignified exit, and Nick smiled with obvious enjoyment of her discomfiture. His voice as smooth as silk, he suggested, "Wouldn't you like to slip into something more comfortable?"

"Yes!"

She sounded so desperate that he let her off the hook. Nodding and turning his back on her, he sauntered to the sofa and began riffling through the newspaper Jamie had left on the coffee table. When Abby remained seated at the piano, he glanced at her, his eyes glinting mischievously as they wandered over her.

"You'd better get a move on," he cautioned, "because I won't be responsible for what happens if you're still sitting there dressed like that five seconds from now."

Having given fair warning, he turned away again and began counting. "One . . . two . . . three . . ."

The steely determination in Nick's intonation of the numbers prompted Abby's reaction. Leaping to her feet, she bolted from the living room before Nick had counted to four.

CHAPTER EIGHT

Alone in her bedroom, taking a cue from the way Nick
was dressed, Abby pulled a denim pantsuit and a candy-
striped blouse out of her closet. She scrambled into the
clothes in record time.

"Where are we going?" she asked as Nick helped her
into the pickup.

"Mt. Horeb," he replied. "There's some property near
the town I'm interested in buying."

Neither of them talked very much during the drive to
the small farming community, which was about twenty
miles west of Madison. When they had left the city behind,
Abby noticed that although the wind carried the scent of
rain, and thunderheads were massing on the horizon, the
clouds were silver-lined. This seemed a good omen and she
decided lightheartedly that her qualms about seeing Nick
today were groundless. There was no place she would
rather be than here with him.

They reached the outskirts of Mt. Horeb and Nick
turned off the highway onto a secondary road that mean-
dered through the gently rolling countryside. After they
had traveled perhaps five miles, he turned again, leaving

the county trunk for a private gravel road that led to a cluster of farm buildings.

From a distance the farmstead was picturesque, but as they drew nearer it became apparent to Abby that while the house seemed habitable, the outbuildings were dilapidated. Some of them looked as if the next high wind would cause them to collapse.

"Isn't it awfully run-down?" she asked.

"It's the land I'm interested in," said Nick. "According to the ad, this acreage yields bumper crops of corn and soybeans."

He braked the pickup to a stop, parking it beneath a huge box elder that spread its branches over the horseshoe drive that served both the house and the barn.

"Wait here," Nick instructed. Lithely unfolding his big frame, he stepped out of the cab. He rummaged around in the back of the truck for a few seconds, and when he appeared at the passenger door, he was carrying a pair of knee-high rubber boots.

"Charming!" Abby declared facetiously. "Did you bring me all the way out here just to show me those?"

Nick glanced disparagingly at her cork-soled sandals. "I should have thought to tell you to wear sensible footgear. You'd better put these on over your shoes."

"But they're so big." She studied the boots dubiously. "I'm not sure I can keep them on, even over my shoes."

"I stuffed the toes with newspaper," Nick advised her briskly. "Give them a try. I think you'll find they're better than what you're wearing. At least they'll keep your feet dry."

Abby complied without further argument, wrinkling her nose with distaste when the boots turned out to be as large and unwieldy as she had feared.

Nick helped her down from the pickup and she hopped first on one foot, then the other, testing whether the boots would stay on when she walked.

Thanks to the newspaper he'd lined them with, they seemed secure enough, if rather awkward. As a final test, she took a few swaggering steps, exaggerating the length of her stride and chanting, "Fee, fi, fo, fum." She stopped with her toes pointed out. Looking down at her feet, she complained, "I feel like a clown."

"From the knees down, you look like one." Nick was trying unsuccessfully to keep from smiling. He quirked an eyebrow at her. "How about it? Are you willing to risk hiking in them?"

"Lead on," she said, waving her hand in a jaunty salute.

Picking her way carefully, she tagged along behind Nick while he made brief tours of what had once been a machine shed and granary. He didn't stop to go inside the poultry house, nor did he investigate several other sheds that were too deteriorated even to be used for storage. He made a more thorough inspection of the dairy barn and milk house, pausing occasionally for a closer look at some antiquated piece of equipment he'd found.

Abby, poking about aimlessly on her own, discovered treasures of another sort: a brave clump of hardy yellow crocuses brightening a shady spot beside a pile of rotting lumber, a swing beneath the apple trees, and the scarlet plumage of a cardinal perched in the branches of the box elder.

Together she and Nick strolled up the driveway to the house, and while Nick searched his pockets for the key the realtor had given him, Abby admired the ripening buds on the lilacs that flanked the steps to the porch.

The farmhouse itself was unremittingly utilitarian and just barely liveable. It had once been the mustard-brown of old train depots, but from the way strips of paint were peeling from its siding, Abby thought it had probably been vacant for quite a number of years, and the tattered shades at the windows confirmed her assumption.

124

"If you decide to buy the place, would you live here?" she asked Nick.

"Hardly." Nick chuckled and threw open the door of the front room to reveal the sacks of seed and fertilizer that were crammed into that part of the house. "No," he said slowly as he wandered along the hall opening doors and glancing into rooms as he passed them. "If I buy it, it would be strictly as an investment. Unless I were lucky enough to find someone who was able and willing to manage it for me, I'd lease the land."

He stopped just outside the kitchen. "Watch your step here," he counseled, batting cobwebs out of the way with his forearm as he entered the room, and stepping over the rubbish that littered the floor. In the center of the kitchen he stopped again and stood staring at the old-fashioned woodburning stove.

"Will you look at that! It must have come over on the ark!" Nick exclaimed.

Abby nodded. "I'll bet an antique buff would pay a tidy sum for it though." Attempting to get a closer look at an oak pedestal table, she squeezed between Nick and a roll of tar paper. "In fact," she added when she spotted a saltcellar the tar paper had concealed, "this room is full of collectibles."

She began searching for antiques in earnest now, and she found nothing further of interest. From the number of old beer cans that were lying around, she could guess how the place had gotten to be so run down.

When Nick suggested they take a walk out to the fields, she was happy to leave the dust and cobwebs of the house behind and go out into the fresh country air.

As cumbersome as the boots were, she was grateful for them when Nick set off down a dirt track that gave access to the fields. The ground was soft and slushy from the thaw. In places there was standing water that was deep enough to swirl about her ankles. At one especially treacherous spot she sank into the mire so deeply that she hadn't enough leverage to pull the boots out.

"Hey, Gabriel," she called loudly but without animosity after Nick, who was walking some distance ahead. He turned and she shook her fist at him, feigning righteous indignation.

"Now I know why you brought me here. You wanted a human scarecrow for your cornfield."

"If that's an offer, it's a hard one to refuse."

Laughing at her plight, Nick came to her rescue, but even with his assistance it was impossible to work her feet out of the bog. Saying "Don't worry, I haven't lost a scarecrow yet," Nick lifted her out of the boots and carried her to the far side of the pothole, setting her down to wait while he retrieved the boots. He tugged at the tops until they came free of the mud with wet, sucking sounds. By the time he joined her on dry ground, both of them were liberally spattered with mud and laughing helplessly.

Between fits of giggles, Abby gasped, "Honestly, Nick, you should see yourself!"

"I'd rather look at you!" He searched his jacket pockets and produced a bandanna from one of them with a flourish. The bandanna was old and so badly faded that in places the red-and-black print was just a memory, but it was clean.

"Ah, ha!" Abby cried. "I see you anticipated this sort of thing might happen."

"My motto is 'Be Prepared.' " Cupping her chin with one hand, Nick began dabbing at the worst of the grime on her face, and helped her put her boots on.

"What else do you have in your pockets?"

"Damned if I know. I haven't worn this coat for a while." Leering down at her, he inquired, "Would you care to search me?"

Abby pretended to consider this. "Maybe later," she replied, leering back at him.

126

"Promises, promises," he said dolefully. He dropped a kiss on her nose and another at the corner of her mouth before he released her.

He mopped at his own face with the bandanna, and they continued on, walking hand in hand.

"What would you grow here?" she asked.

"If I buy the place, I'd probably switch over to tobacco, so I wouldn't have much use for a scarecrow."

"Tobacco?" Abby repeated quizzically. "That seems a natural for an ex-baseball player." She glanced up at him, trying to imagine his cleanly chiseled features distorted by a wad of the stuff in his cheek. "Did you ever chew?"

He grinned down at her. "Tobacco, you mean?"

She nodded.

"No, Abby, I didn't, except for one time when I was about Jamie's age. A bunch of my buddies and I found a package of Star chewing tobacco and experimented with it. I guess we thought it would do more than bubble gum to make us seem grownup, but all it did was make us sick." He shook his head ruefully. "I've never been so sick, before that time or since."

"I wonder if Jamie has ever tried something like that."

"If he has, would you really want to know about it?" asked Nick.

"No, I suppose I wouldn't," she answered faintly. "Not if it ended with the one trial."

"From the way you say that, I gather you did your own share of experimenting when you were a teen-ager."

"Didn't we all?"

They had come to a fence line and Nick held the wire so she could crawl under it, then she returned the favor for him. Now they were crossing an open field that led to a knoll, and the going was more difficult than before.

For a time Abby walked without speaking, keeping her eyes fixed on the path they were following and shaken by the sudden chill she felt as she recalled her own misguided attempts to assert her independence. It was not as if they'd amounted to much, but they might have.

Since she'd been a casualty of the open warfare between her parents, it had been unthinkable to her to engage in shouting matches with her mother. Her acts of defiance had necessarily been more covert.

· She'd sneaked out a few times to circumvent her mother's curfew. She had tried cigarettes and liquor, but she'd found that smoking made her cough, alcohol put her to sleep, and an excess of either of them left her nauseated. She'd petted a bit too, enough to learn that fumbling kisses, adolescent gropings, and heavy breathing in the backseats of cars didn't really qualify as high romance.

Sighing, Abby picked up the thread of the conversation with Nick. "It's just that I hate to think of Jamie wanting to rush into adulthood and going through the same hassles some of my friends and I did.

"Besides," she added heatedly, "there are so many dangerous drugs available to kids nowadays, and they're subjected to so much peer pressure to give them a try. There are a frightening number of youngsters who have ruined their lives before they're even old enough to know what they're risking, and what makes it even more insidious is that it's all to satisfy the greed of some contemptible crook!"

As soon as the words were out, Abby wished she could retract them, for Nick let go of her hand.

"Jamie will be all right," he said shortly, quickening his pace so that he was striding ahead of her across the field. "He has to grow up sometime, and if you don't let him go gracefully, you'll lose him."

"Look," she cried, "I apologize for being tactless, but please, Nick, believe me when I say that my remarks about narcotics weren't premeditated. It's just that I forgot about the charges—"

"I believe you."

Nick kept on walking and after a few clumsy steps, Abby realized it was futile to try to keep up with him. She slowed, then stopped completely. Thinking that he might prefer some time alone to cool off, she called after him, "I'll wait for you here."

"See you in a few minutes then," he replied dismissively.

She had hoped Nick would insist she accompany him, but he didn't even turn around to look at her. She was disappointed again when she waited for him to offer a friendly gesture of farewell, following him with her eyes until his retreating figure had become a featureless silhouette against the cloudy sky. Only when he had disappeared into the copse of trees at the top of the hill did she begin working her way back to the road.

Surely Nick's reaction was way out of proportion to her chance comment, thoughtless though it had been. She felt rotten for having reminded him of his legal problems, but she had tried to apologize. What more did he expect?

She crossed under the fence on her own, snagging her jacket on the barbed wire in the process. This additional nuisance fueled her resentment.

"*Mea culpa,*" she muttered sarcastically as she sat down on a slab of rock on the far side of the road to wait for him.

Her presence flushed a ground squirrel from his burrow beneath the rock. The little animal sat on his haunches at the entrance to his home and studied her inquisitively.

"Good Lord, but he's touchy!" Abby offered this opinion to the ground squirrel, startling him so that he scampered back into his tunnel, leaving her alone with her thoughts.

In retrospect she decided that much as she regretted her blunder, it had a certain redeeming value. She knew now that Nick's attitude toward the criminal charges that had been made against him was less sanguine than he let on. It was fairly obvious that he wasn't as detached as she had thought. And if he cared about that, maybe he cared about other things as well.

Nick was gone more than a few minutes. It was closer to half an hour before he returned. He was gone long enough for Abby's irritation to fade, long enough that she spent the last anxious minutes recalling how fast he'd been walking over the rutted surface of the field, how he'd been scaling obstacles rather than going around them when he'd climbed the rougher terrain of the hillside. He was gone long enough that she began worrying that he might have reinjured his knee.

She peered at the lowering sky apprehensively, wondering if Nick would be back in time to prevent their being caught in the open by a thunderstorm. The towering bank of clouds that had begun to accumulate shortly after noon was now almost directly overhead, illuminated by intermittent flashes of lightning.

Nick and the storm arrived simultaneously. Thunder crashed nearby and just as the first drops of rain fell, he came into view. He vaulted the fence and jogged toward her, smiling his devastating smile when he saw that she was still waiting for him and looking for all the world as if he had personally commanded the elements.

"Let's go!" he called. Without breaking stride he grabbed her hand and pulled her along in his wake.

The wind at their backs swept them along as they ran through the rain, retracing the way they had come. Nick's high-spirited enjoyment of the weather was infectious, and Abby laughed with him. Even when she was out of breath and bothered by a stitch in her side, she couldn't stop laughing.

She stumbled over the boots several times before they reached the farmstead, but this only increased their hilarity. Finally, when she had fallen into Nick and almost brought both of them down, he scooped her up in his arms as if she were weightless and carried her the rest of the way to the barn.

He put her down, unzipped his jacket, and drew her inside, and they stood in the open doorway with their arms around each other, sharing their body heat and gauging the approach of the storm by the color of the sky.

Just before the deluge hit, the air took on a strange, greenish cast and the wind lashed at the branches of the box elder. At the height of the downpour the rain was so heavy that they were unable to see the house, although it was only a few hundred feet beyond the tree.

"God, but there's something about a thunderstorm!" Nick shouted elatedly, tipping his head back to catch the rain in his mouth.

Abby smiled up at him, delighting in his boyish exuberance, happy because he was happy, content because he held her in his arms.

"You should do this more often," said Nick.

Her expression was suddenly solemn. "Do what?" she asked, mystified.

He touched the frown lines between her eyebrows, erasing them. "Smile," he said softly. "Laugh. Shout if you feel like it. Get mad. Stop trying to be something you're not." His attention shifted to her lips and he turned her mouth up at the corners with his forefinger. His mouth was only a fraction of an inch away from her own, and his eyes probed hers as he smoothed the wind-tossed hair away from her forehead. "Take whatever comes and make the most of it. Enjoy . . ."

Nick left the sentence unfinished, replacing his words with actions. He kissed Abby, and it seemed to her that she had been waiting all her life for this moment. She had never known how cool and silky rain could feel until she felt its dampness on his face, never known its he sweet-ness until she'd tasted it on his lips. It was i
but it seemed to her that she had been crea'

the hungry pressure of his mouth, to receive the demanding thrust of his lips.

In an instant of revelation her commitment was made, her fate sealed. A soul-destroying wave of longing rushed through her, but this turbulent response seemed a natural extension of the storm raging outside.

When Nick released her, she tried to move away from him, but she staggered and almost fell.

His arm went around her waist to steady her and she leaned against him, thankful for his support as he guided her deeper into the dusky cavern of the barn. He found some burlap feed sacks for her to sit on while he removed the boots and, watching him, Abby choked back a hysterical bubble of laughter.

Much as she might wish they were the cause, her momentary weakness had nothing to do with the boots she was wearing. She had faltered because she was giddy with reaction, shaken by the knowledge that her doubts and unanswered questions about Nick were no longer relevant. Like it or not, she was in love with him.

She closed her eyes, but his face was indelibly etched in her mind. She might try to deny she loved him, she might try to ignore her feelings, but there was no turning back. She would never be able to forget this moment, much less banish the recognition of her love for Nick.

She would always remember this tumbledown barn with the rain drumming on its leaky roof. When she was very old, the scratchy texture of burlap, the sweet yet pungent odor of hay would conjure up the memory of this isolated moment in time when she realized she was in love with Nick.

Suddenly Abby sneezed, and her eyes opened a bit in surprise that her body could continue to function as it usually did when her emotions had undergone such an upheaval. She glanced at Nick from beneath her lashes and saw that he was still sitting on his heels in front of her, holding the boots in one hand. Wide-eyed now, she looked at him, but her eyes were soft and unfocused until she became aware that he had spoken to her.

"Wh-what did you say?" she inquired.

"I said the rain's stopped, and I asked if you want to leave now."

She stared at him numbly.

"Are you all right?"

How could she answer that? She was totally disoriented. Her world was spinning off its axis and she wasn't sure she would survive the cataclysm. She wanted to laugh. She wanted to weep. But she didn't do either.

Instead she reached out and brushed back the tawny shock of hair that had fallen across Nick's forehead. Then she put out her other hand and removed an apple blossom that was tangled in the sun-bleached strands at the crown of his head. She ran her hands over his face, tracing the slant of his eyebrows, the angle of his cheekbones, the bold jut of his chin, cherishing him with her fingertips, loving him with her eyes, not hesitating until she arrived at his mouth.

He was saying something to her, but she only saw his lips move. Of their own volition her arms were entwined around his neck. She was drawing him toward her and molding her lips to his.

Surprised, Nick held back at first, letting her take the initiative. But when she outlined his upper lip with the tip of her tongue, his arms went around her. She approached the barrier of his teeth shyly, and his hands moved to her waist to pull her closer to the sheltering curve of his body. He cupped her breasts in his hands and gently shaped them within his palms, encouraging her to make new advances, urging her on to greater intimacies.

At this sweet provocation her tongue slipped through the line of his teeth to challenge his tongue to an amorous duel. Her shyness was forgotten as she explored the roof of his mouth, the insides of his cheeks, searching out the deepest, most intoxicating contours of his mouth. Not satisfied with this, she drew his lower lip between her own lips and nibbled at it playfully, savoring the taste of his mouth as if she would seduce him with a single kiss.

She felt his body harden until it was as tightly drawn as a bowstring against her own. His eyes were dazed and dark with passion when she finally moved away from him.

"My God!" he exclaimed shakily. "What's gotten into you? Where did you learn that little trick?"

"T-trick?" For a moment she was bewildered, then she laughed throatily and teased, "What's wrong, Nick? Are you afraid my intentions are dishonorable?"

His hands tightened around her waist, and he lifted her to her feet, pulling her into his arms with an urgency that made her senses reel.

"Abby, sweetheart," he growled, "I sincerely hope they are."

CHAPTER NINE

Abby tugged at the neckline of her blouse, adjusting it so that it revealed more of the creamy swell of her breasts. The peasant-style blouse was of white organza, its only ornamentation the frothy elasticized ruffle that allowed it to be worn either on or off the shoulder.

Now that the garment rode an inch or so lower, she wondered if she was being too obvious. Studying the effect in the mirror, she turned this way and that, and the lining of her black velvet evening skirt swished about her legs with a sibilant whisper that made her feel very feminine and a little wicked.

The skirt was the perfect choice for tonight, but she wasn't at all certain about the blouse. With the neckline raised it was too demure. With it lowered she looked blatantly provocative.

It was the ruffle that did it, she decided, pulling the neckline higher so that less of her was exposed. Because the rest of her was so slender, her full breasts made her appear voluptuous to begin with. The added ruffle only emphasized this.

Still pondering her appearance, she dabbed perfume

behind her earlobes, on her throat, and in the hollow between her breasts. Her hands were shaking so badly that she almost tipped the bottle over when she replaced the stopper.

She hadn't been so jittery at the prospect of spending an evening with a man since she was a teen-ager preparing for her first date. And she didn't truly have a date with Nick tonight, at least not in the conventional sense of the word.

When they'd returned from Mt. Horeb and he'd dropped her at her front door, Nick hadn't asked her to join him at the main house for dinner. He'd told her.

Nick had made his intentions plain long before he'd held her in his arms at the farmhouse, so it was no wonder she felt tonight's meeting was half command performance, half assignation. Both of them knew that by keeping the rendezvous with him she was tacitly agreeing to something much more intimate than a casual dinner date.

Maybe it would be better to change into a more modest blouse, thought Abby.

A feeling closely akin to panic set her heart racing as she crossed the bedroom and opened the closet. She had already reached for a lacy, high-necked Edwardian blouse when she stopped.

Her actions reminded her of Lucinda Mooney, one of her friends from high-school days. Lucinda had often loudly condemned the girls in their class who were known to be sleeping with their boyfriends. Just as loudly she had proclaimed that she was "saving herself for her one true love," the man she would someday marry. But when the captain of the football team or some other equally sought-after young swain had asked Lucinda out, her much-vaunted virtue hadn't stopped her from donning her sexiest undies for their date, "just in case."

Abby supposed a certain amount of hypocrisy was not a bad thing. She supposed that it helped to keep people from running completely amok. But who was she trying to deceive?

If she changed her blouse, she would be fooling no one. Not Nick, and certainly not herself.

She had known almost from the beginning where their relationship was heading. When Nick had said they both knew what they wanted, she'd even admitted as much to him. No matter how hard she tried, she couldn't conceal how desperately she wanted him.

Her appearance tonight virtually shrieked it. Desire had brought uncharacteristic color to her face. She looked as if she were wearing gobs of makeup when, in fact, she hadn't applied any. Her lips were rosy, her cheeks vivid, and her amber eyes were shadowed and mysterious without artifice. Even her hair sparkled with new highlights.

She was keenly aware of her body too, for while she'd been showering and getting into fresh clothing, with one part of herself she had been observing herself as Nick might, and she wondered whether she could live up to his expectations. Hence she felt self-consciousness about the way she was dressed.

With a shrug that caused her blouse to slip lower on her shapely shoulders, Abby closed the closet door.

If she kept her engagement with Nick, it was better to be honest with herself. She was not a silly teen-ager. She was a mature woman of nearly twenty-eight, and it was high time she behaved like one.

Still, after she had picked up her coat and evening bag from the foot of the bed, she stopped to check her appearance in the mirror one last time. When she saw how low the ruffle had slipped, she settled on a compromise. She removed the white silk rose she'd pinned in her hair and tucked it between her breasts. Feeling slightly less wanton, she left the cottage.

Dinner was simple but delicious. The steak was perfectly broiled, the Caesar salad crisp and piquantly seasoned, the rolls crusty and aromatic. Although she was too excited to do justice to the meal, Abby thought that food had never tasted so good. But then, tonight it seemed that all her senses were tuned to an exquisite pitch.

She was capable of discerning the subtlest variations in tastes and textures, in scents and colors. Nick's eyes were such an extraordinary blue, it caused a strange ache inside her just to look at them. Because of her training in music, she was always supersensitive to sounds, but tonight she could almost swear she heard the wax dripping from the lighted tapers on the dinner table.

As they lingered at the table finishing the last of a bottle of wine, the world contracted until everything was excluded but the small circle of candlelight that encompassed Nick and her. Under the relaxing influence of the wine, Abby flirted shamelessly with Nick and congratulated herself on how convincingly she was playing the unfamiliar role of a woman with vast experience in conducting love affairs. But no sooner had she done this than Nick asked, "Where's Jamie tonight?" and her composure temporarily deserted her.

She took a fortifying sip of wine before she answered, but it might as well have been water. Distinguished though the vintage was, she was no longer capable of appreciating the mellow Beaujolais. In the safety of her own bedroom it had been comparatively easy to decide that, if Nick wanted her to, she would spend the night with him, but now that the moment was at hand, she was not nearly as certain this choice was the right one.

To ease her nervousness she offered to help Nick clear the table, but he declined, grinning with a maddening significance that told her he sensed her misgivings, and that he knew she was playing for time. Balancing the coffee tray with one hand, he linked his free arm with hers, clasped her hand with a firmness that said he would not take no for an answer, and suggested that they adjourn to the music room for dessert. Her trepidations multiplied when they arrived there and she saw how thoroughly Nick had set the scene for seduction.

A fire blazed in the hearth of the opulent cream and dusty-rose room. There was music playing softly on the stereo, the lamps were adjusted so that the room was dimly lit and, as if nature had joined forces with Nick, the rain had started again, not violently this time, but with a gentle patter that underscored how romantic it was that the two of them were alone in this cozy room, that they were sheltered from the elements, safe from intrusion, protected from prying eyes.

Acting on her first impulse, Abby sat in one of the wing chairs near the fireplace. Except to smile while he passed her a cup of coffee and a serving of The Boulangerie's famous cheesecake, Nick made no comment on her choice. He sat in the chair opposite her, watching as, with the smallest possible bites, she ate the dessert.

When it became apparent that he was only having coffee, she asked, "A-aren't you going to try the cheese-cake?"

"I'll have my dessert later," he replied evenly.

"It's awfully good," she enthused, shaken by the double entendre. "Amaretto, isn't it?"

Nick nodded.

"That's my very favorite liqueur." The cheesecake was delectable. The only trouble was that he'd served her the merest sliver and it was almost gone. Taking another tack, she said brightly, "Jamie told me you'd let him see some of your original drawings for 'Sebastian.' Where do you work?"

"I've set up a studio in one of the guest rooms."

Abby had thought simple courtesy would require that

he offer to show her his drawings, but all he offered was that terse statement.

She ate the last crumb of the cake and stared forlornly at the empty plate before setting it aside. Trying to appear nonchalant, she toyed with the electrical cord of the lamp on the table beside her, finally switching it on. She regretted this almost immediately, for now that the light was brighter, Nick's scrutiny of her became even more intent.

"That's remarkable," he exclaimed softly.

Her hand fluttered nervously to her throat. "What is?"

"Your skin. It shimmers as if it's been sprinkled with gold dust."

"Oh, that," she replied in a brittle voice that devalued the extravagance of the compliment. "It's from a lotion, actually. It's called Liquid Gold."

"It's very effective." His eyes left her face to wander over her shoulders and arms, lingering on her breasts. "Do you use it all over?"

Her cup rattled in its saucer. "S-sometimes." She took a sip of coffee, hoping it would steady her. "Gordon gave it to me last Christmas," she added shakily. "He thought, since I'm so pale, it might make me look a bit healthier."

Tonight she had used the lotion thinking it might tone down the unusually high color in her face. It hadn't.

Abby lowered her eyes to concentrate on the dregs of coffee remaining in her cup and wondered how it had come to be empty so soon. She had no recollection of drinking it.

She was unaware that Nick had gotten to his feet until he reached for her cup. She glanced up at him and was startled by the uncompromising set of his jaw. It made him look aggressive and threatening. Her own grip on the saucer tightened and a silent tug-of-war ensued.

"M-may I have more coffee?" she asked.

"If you really want it." The impact of his gaze was almost tangible and his nearness was devastating. Her fingers went limp and the cup slipped from her grasp. With an air of finality, Nick replaced it on the coffee tray and turned to face her.

If anyone had asked, Abby couldn't have said what was playing on the stereo, but in a feeble attempt to forestall Nick, she observed, "The music is lovely."

"Would you like to dance?" Nick promptly returned.

She realized her tactical error when, without waiting for her to reply, he drew her to her feet and led her away from the light and into the shadows at the center of the room. His arms went around her and his hands swept over her back, pulling her close, lifting her onto her tiptoes and folding her closer still.

Weak-kneed, Abby clung to Nick with her arms around his neck. He swayed in time to the music, but he made no pretense of dancing. With nearly imperceptible movements of his hands at the small of her back, he molded her to him until she was acutely conscious of the erotic pressure of his hips against hers.

"I like your perfume," he whispered close to her ear.

"It's the same brand as the lotion," she murmured. "It's called Pheromone."

"Pheromone?" he repeated incredulously, raising his head to smile lazily down at her. "I thought that was something female insects used to lure male insects to them."

"Th-that's right, but the perfume is only named for it. Jamie says if I'm not careful, I'll attract every bee in the county."

Nick laughed deep in his throat and rubbed his cheek against hers. "Buzz-z-z," he growled, stinging the side of her neck with little biting kisses.

Desperately trying to slow his headlong assault on her senses, Abby blurted out, "Gordon gave me the perfume too."

"Gordon!"

At this gratuitous bit of information, Nick's grip on her tightened until his hands were digging almost painfully into her sides. Then, resuming his slow erosion of her inhibitions, his hands left her waist to skim lightly over her midriff and caress the bare skin of her shoulders.

Although his hold on her had loosened, it was beyond Abby to make the effort to put any distance between them. Instead her hands slid up the muscular column of his neck to cradle his head. She let her body flow into his and tipped her head back so that they were standing cheek to cheek.

He nuzzled her ear, nibbling at the lobe and delving into the recesses with the tip of his tongue until her skin grew pebbly with gooseflesh at the delightful sensations he was evoking and she began to tremble.

"Did Gordon ever do this to you?" he demanded silkily.

"N-no," she answered weakly.

His lips moved beguilingly, exploring the soft, pulsing hollows at the base of her throat.

"Or this?"

"No. N-never."

Now he was trailing kisses over her shoulders and across the rise of her breasts, following the décolletage of the blouse. When he arrived at the silk rose, he stopped.

"How about this?" he drawled. The backs of his fingers grazed her breasts as he slid the rose out of its resting place, and she flinched as if scalded by his touch.

She was, at the same time, stunned by his insolence and baffled by his preoccupation over her relationship with Gordon. Incapable of speech, she could only shake her head helplessly.

It seemed he was satisfied with her reply, however. Before he tossed the rose aside, he pressed the flower to his lips. It was as if he were kissing her, and her breathing quickened alarmingly. Holding her chin in his hand to keep her still, he brushed her mouth with his in a gentle prying motion that coaxed her lips to part. He felt the shuddering sigh that signaled her capitulation, and at the next instant her mouth opened, yielding its sweetness to the hard demand of his mouth.

He claimed the prize of victory as if he savored the act of conquest, now advancing, now retreating, slowly deepening his invasion until she returned the hot probing of his tongue with her own fiery ardor. Abby had never tasted passion fruit, but surely that must be what Nick tasted of—that or something equally delicious and exotic and sinfully desirable.

Her hands were clutching at his shirt front, searching for buttons, becoming frantic when she found none, and when she remembered that his shirt buttoned only at the collar, she almost whimpered with frustration before she discovered she could slide her hands underneath the tail. She ran her hands over his back, learning how warm his skin was and how smooth, as smooth as silk tightly stretched over the flat, steely ridges of muscle.

Then, just when her senses were clamoring for more, Nick released her.

He moved away from her slightly, and when she swayed as if to follow him, he deliberately kept her at bay with his hands on her upper arms.

She looked up at him dazedly, bewildered by his sudden withdrawal, not knowing why he had stopped making love to her. She knew he wanted her. She had felt the hard surge of his desire. Even now his needs were communicated by the fine tremor in his hands as he ran his palms up and down her arms in a light, repetitive caress.

"Abby," he said thickly, "if you're planning to leave here tonight, now is the time."

She made a small sound of protest. How could she bear

to leave him now? Again she tried to close the gap between them, and again he fended her off. Confused, she studied the austere cast of his features. His mouth was compressed to a determined line, and his surveillance of her was so piercing, it seemed to penetrate to the very core of her being.

"I want to hear you say it," Nick persisted.

What did he want to hear? She wanted to shout that she loved him, that she wanted him, but intuition warned her to choose a more cautious response. She heard herself say, "I want to stay, Nick," and she was rewarded by the brilliance of his smile as his arms went around her, catching her in a bone-crushing hug that took her breath away.

Nick's breathing was labored too. His voice was ragged with desire as he said, "God, Abby! Have you any idea how much I want you?"

He whispered small endearments against her lips before he buried her mouth with his, kissing her as if he were starved for her. Once again he ran his hands along her arms, but this time they tangled with the ruffle on her blouse, impatiently pulling it lower. Her limbs were languid and heavy, and she stood as if rooted to the carpet while he unhooked her bra, freeing her full, rounded breasts.

She longed for him to hold her, she ached for his touch, but he only looked at her hungrily and murmured, "You're so beautiful."

Unable to bear the emotion she saw in his face, she closed her eyes, and the suspense of waiting spun out electrically until, at last, she felt his hands upon her. His fingers feathered over her nipples, generating a primitive shock wave of desire that left her gasping.

"Soft," he whispered hoarsely, "so soft. And lovely. More beautiful than I'd imagined."

Desperate for his embrace, she worked her arms out of

the blouse and blindly reached for him. Even while he continued fondling her, her questing hands found his chest. When she realized he had removed his shirt, her eyes opened wide to drink in his hard, masculine beauty. She touched him tentatively at first, but his sharp intake of breath encouraged her to become bolder, to caress the powerful width of his shoulders, the patch of fine tawny fuzz that arrowed from his rugged chest to his flat belly. She arrived at the waistband of his slacks and her caresses moved lower, searching for new parts of him to explore, eagerly filling her hands with his glory.

Her heart was thudding violently, drowning out any sound other than the feverish rush of blood through her veins, but she sensed the deep rumble of Nick's groan as he crushed her to him.

He lifted her in his arms and carried her out of the music room, up the stairs, and into his bedroom, handling her so effortlessly that she felt she must be floating. But she knew she couldn't be because the mattress dipped beneath her weight as he laid her on the bed.

Hurriedly Nick peeled away the rest of her clothes and stood by the bed to strip off his own. She lay where he had left her, waiting in expectant silence while vague rustling sounds told her of his progress. She wished she dared search for the bedside lamp. She wanted to see him, but it was so dark in the room that no matter how she strained her eyes, all she could make out was the faint glimmer of his skin.

Then he stretched out beside her, gathering her close again, and everything else was forgotten. There was blissful oblivion in his taut nakedness, in the sweet domination of his kisses, in the touch of his hands as he learned the silky contours of her body.

Her own explorations grew more reckless, more intimate, and when he discovered secret places and caressed

145

her wildly, she felt herself melting and blossoming.

He wrapped his arms and legs around her and arched her into his kisses while his lips followed a course from her throat to her breasts. His tongue flicked over the nipples, teasing them until they were erect and tingling, and when she moaned with pleasure, he uttered a low sound of triumph at her response.

"Did Gordon ever do this?" he whispered harshly.

Reluctant to be shaken from her rapture, Abby didn't reply, but the bright, sensuous glow of desire began to fade.

"Did he?" Nick repeated, his voice softly insistent.

She shivered at the coldness of his interrogation and answered with an automatic shake of her head.

He rolled her over so that she was on her back and he was lying on top of her, pressing her deep into the bed-clothes with the force of his passion.

"Has Gordon done this?" he muttered, but Abby didn't hear the question. In the same moment he asked it, she involuntarily stiffened and Nick's eager movements stopped.

"My God! He hasn't, has he?" Nick stared down at her, finding his answer in the tense whiteness of her face. "Oh, sweet Jesus, Abby! Neither has anyone else!"

He eased his weight off of her, turning onto his side and taking her with him so that they still lay with their legs entwined.

"Why didn't you tell me?" he asked, his voice gruff with concern.

"What difference would it have made?" she returned warily.

"Well, for one thing, I wouldn't have wasted so much time worrying that I might be poaching on another man's territory."

"It seems to me you've wasted precious little time as it

is. Anyway, it's not something I'm especially proud of—not in this day and age—and even if I were, it's rather awkward to work that kind of thing into everyday conversation."

Recognizing her arguments as the smokescreen they were, Nick smiled at her and said, "You were embarrassed."

Although she heard the note of tenderness in his voice, she reacted to his assumption by burying her face in the curve of his shoulder.

"You're still embarrassed," he declared, and this time she nodded.

Tugging gently at her hair, Nick forced her to tip her head back so he could see her face. "You shouldn't be. You're very beautiful." His hands were moving over her again, telling her just how beautiful he thought she was. "Besides," he added, chuckling a little, "this is a first for me too."

Her jaw dropped with disbelief and Nick closed her mouth with a gentle push of his knuckles on the point of her chin. He dropped a light kiss on her forehead and his lips brushed her skin as he whispered, "It's true, sweet Abby. I've never made love to a virgin before."

With a shaky little laugh, Abby relaxed in his arms. Snuggling closer to him, she admitted shyly, "I was afraid you might not want me if you knew."

"Not want you!" With a lithe twist of his body, Nick pinned her beneath him again. His hands clutched at her hips, welding her to him and offering irrefutable proof that her fears were unjustified. "Abby, love," he said roughly, "before very much longer, I intend to show you just how much I want you."

The intimate way he was holding her had already rekindled her desires. He began touching her with a compelling urgency, as if he would never have enough of her, and suddenly she was on fire for him, consumed with need for him.

"Please, Nick," she pleaded huskily. "Show me now."

No further invitation was necessary. With a fierce growl of pleasure and an unbridled passion that catapulted her to the tumultuous heights of ecstasy, Nick granted her request.

CHAPTER TEN

"Is it always like this?"

Nick's chuckle was a deep, throaty rumble that sounded almost as if he were purring. When Abby felt his chest vibrate beneath her cheek, her lips curved into a smile of utter contentment.

"No, not always." The blend of tenderness and gratification in Nick's voice was as revealing as his answer. It told her he was more than a little pleased with himself because he had induced her to respond so unrestrainedly to his lovemaking. But what was more important was that she knew he was pleased with her.

He was cradling her close, her head resting on his chest, and with every passing second she could feel his arms about her growing heavier with relaxation.

Abby was drowsy too, but she was also oddly exhilarated and nearly light-headed with euphoria. She rubbed her cheek against his chest, delighting in the texture of his skin. He smelled of something spicy and virile and faintly musky, except for the nape of his neck, which held the slightest trace of barber's talc, and his hands, which smelled of soap and of Abby.

She was surprised by how comfortably their bodies fit together, astonished that a man so big and angular could be so cuddly. She had never been so close to anyone before. She had never felt so open, as if she could let down her guard completely and share her innermost thoughts and feelings with Nick, and not be at all self-conscious. She longed to know everything there was to know about him. She wanted to know how he'd gotten the scar on his eyebrow, and whether he had any relatives other than his brother Hank, and how he happened to be so knowledgeable about classical music. She wanted to know how he'd gotten interested in drawing, and whether he liked a big, cooked breakfast, and if he preferred summer or winter vacations.

Hoping to prolong their intimacy, she confided, "I wasn't expecting it to be so wonderful."

"You're a witch, Ab-by." He drew her name out sweetly. "I could swear I've died and gone to heaven, and you're making me feel about ten feet tall, but it takes two."

"You're not disappointed?"

"You know damned well I'm not," Nick returned good-naturedly, "so why are you fishing for compliments?"

"I'm not sure that I am," she replied slowly. "I think it's just that I've heard so many conflicting reports about sex. Oh, I've known the biological facts from the classes I had in high school, but they were presented so, well, so clinically. And my mother would never discuss the subject with me. I tried several times to ask her questions, but all she'd say was that we'd talk about it tomorrow, or next week, or when she thought I was ready."

Abby sighed deeply. "She never got around to it though. I guess she found it embarrassing or something, but the impression she gave was that sex wasn't a topic nice people talked about. And kids being what they are, that hint of sinfulness made me more curious than ever.

150

For a while I was so preoccupied with sex, I thought there must be something wrong with me."

Nick pressed his lips against her hair and ran his hand from her waist to her hips, stopping warmly when he reached her thigh. "Well, now you know there isn't," he whispered sleepily.

"Yes, now I do," she murmured, "but at the time, it was very confusing. A lot of girls at school talked about very little but sex and boys. Some of them even compared notes and tried to top each other about how experienced they were in bed, but it was obvious they were trying to impress the other girls with their sophistication, so I discounted their stories by about fifty percent.

"Finally I decided that it must be pretty normal for a teen-ager to think about sex constantly. I mean, your body is maturing and you're discovering your own sexuality, so I suppose it's only natural." After a thoughtful silence she added, "I suppose it's the same for boys."

"Mmmph," Nick mumbled, and she interpreted this an affirmative reply.

"Of course"—Abby paused to stifle a yawn—"movies are fairly explicit nowadays, and so are books, but until tonight I thought they were exaggerating."

Her eyelids were so heavy she could barely keep them open, but there was something she had to say to Nick before she fell asleep.

"I've never felt so proud to be a woman as I am right now, and it's because of you, Nick. When I'm with you I feel desirable and happy and complete. I just wanted you to know that." She hesitated briefly before concluding in a rush, "And I want you to know how very much I love you."

There, she'd said it!

Abby held her breath, waiting for Nick's reaction. When there was none, she whispered his name, but he still made no acknowledgment. His arms were leaden weights about her. She ran her foot along his lower leg, tracing the solid muscles of his calf, and wriggled her toes against his. Even when she curled her fingers into the mat of hair on his chest and pulled at it gently, he remained inert.

She realized he had dozed off. So, for that matter, had her arm, which was wedged underneath her.

She tried to turn onto her back so she could slip her arm out of the trap between her side and the mattress, but Nick's hold on her tightened, preventing her from moving.

Sighing again, partly with resignation to the growing numbness in her arm and partly with sheer delight, Abby threw her other arm across Nick's chest and closed her eyes. In a few minutes she, too, had drifted off to sleep.

It was a little before midnight when the telephone rang. Still half asleep, Nick fumbled for the receiver and picked it up on the second ring.

Alerted by some sixth sense the instant he'd moved, Abby woke up just as he answered. Initially she was only vaguely aware of Nick's end of the conversation, for he was speaking in muted tones in order not to disturb her. When she stretched luxuriously, rolling onto her back and flexing her arm to restore the circulation to it, Nick felt the shifting of the mattress and realized she was stirring about. He switched on a lamp and consulted the clock on the nightstand.

"At this hour!" he exclaimed rather grumpily. "My God, Hank! Can't it wait till morning?"

Blinking in the unexpected brightness, Abby saw that Nick was sitting on the edge of the bed with his head propped in his hands, holding the receiver in place with his shoulder. As she admired the long line of his back and the bronze smoothness of his skin, Abby recognized that something his brother had said had caused Nick to go rigid with tension. He looked as if he were scowling with his entire body.

Wrapping herself in the sheet, she got to her knees behind him and started massaging the base of his neck. He leaned into her touch to guide her hands to the spots where the kinks were most bothersome, and she began kneading the muscles of his shoulders, loving the supple feel of him beneath her fingers.

"If you just got in, that explains it," Nick remarked. He sounded less irritable now, but his brother's voice had risen excitedly until Abby could make out occasional syllables. She felt the first faint twinge of alarm.

"My understanding was that the situation had been resolved," Nick cut in crisply.

After listening a few seconds longer, he muttered an oath and sprang to his feet. "Hold on a minute," he barked, raking his fingers angrily through his hair. "I want to take this on another phone."

Covering the mouthpiece with his hand, he swiveled to face Abby. Her throat constricted at his anxious expression. Not only did the snatches of conversation she'd overheard constitute grounds for concern, Nick had gone pale.

"This is going to take awhile," he said grimly. "Would you hang up this phone when I pick up the extension?"

Abby nodded and he laid the receiver aside, retrieved his pants which were draped over the end of the bed, and quickly pulled them on.

"Is everything all right?" she asked gravely.

Nick's back was to her again as he zipped his trousers. He didn't respond to her question. He seemed not to have heard it.

"Is there anything else I can do?" She tried again.

"No, nothing," Nick answered shortly as he left the bedroom.

She stared after him worriedly until his voice coming over the phone from the other room reminded her of her promise to hang up the phone.

It was while she was cradling the receiver that she

noticed the photograph of Kirsten on the nightstand. Folding the sheet saronglike around herself, Abby climbed out of bed and wandered about the room collecting discarded articles of clothing from the floor. Purposely keeping busy, she shook the creases out of her skirt and hung it over the back of a chair along with her underwear. Her blouse and brassiere were nowhere to be found, and she continued searching for them until she recalled that they had been left in the music room.

Her heart raced unevenly at the recollection, providing a temporary distraction from the temptation to have a closer look at Kirsten's picture.

The photograph drew her like a magnet while she was gathering up Nick's clothing. By the time that was taken care of, she had worked her way back to the nightstand and was staring at the silver-framed portrait of Nick's wife. Against her will, she reached out and picked it up.

Did Nick keep Kirsten's picture at his bedside, or had the picture of the Baumans' daughter simply been in the room? Abby wondered.

A pang of jealousy shot through her at the thought that Nick possibly still loved her and was followed immediately by a sense of shame. She sank down onto the bed, grasping the frame so tightly that it cut into her fingers.

That she should be envious of a woman who had been dead for three years was bad enough. That the woman was Ben and Peggy's daughter made her envy even more reprehensible.

Abby had met Kirsten only once—when she was an impressionable thirteen and Kirsten was nineteen or twenty—but that one meeting had been sufficient for the older girl to inspire her admiration.

It had been a few months before Jamie was born, shortly after Abby and her mother had moved into the Baumans' guest cottage, that Ben and Peggy had invited them to a farewell party for Kirsten. The hiatus between Bruce Ri-

154

ordans's death and Jamie's birth had been an especially distressing time for her mother and her. Audrey hadn't wanted to go to the party, but Peggy had insisted they attend, so she'd given in.

Although it had been more than fourteen years ago, Abby's memories of the occasion were vivid. She had been sitting at her mother's side, unsure of herself among so many strangers, wanting to join the boisterous carryings-on of the younger people but too shy to make the attempt, when Kirsten had come along and taken her under her wing.

"I hear you play a mean piano, little one," she'd said, "and that's just what this party needs to get it off the ground."

Her voice was naturally husky, with an expressive little catch in it that would melt the hardest heart—or break it. Certainly it was unthinkable that Abby would refuse. To her thirteen-year-old mind, Kirsten Bauman had represented everything that was beautiful and elegant.

Since the party had been in Kirsten's honor, Abby had thought Kirsten would simply introduce her to the crowd of young folk and leave her to fend for herself, but she hadn't. Abby remembered how tactful Kirsten had been, how kind. She'd also been bright and witty, charming and graceful; in fact, the older girl had possessed so many desirable attributes that Abby had been quite overwhelmed by her. Senseless as it was, she supposed she was still overwhelmed by Kirsten.

Later that evening, when the party was over and they had returned to the cottage, Audrey Riordan had reacted petulantly to Abby's praising Kirsten, claiming that Kirsten was willful and spoiled because she'd been cosseted so much following a childhood injury that had nearly cost her life.

Abby dismissed her mother's criticism. With Bruce

gone, Audrey no longer had anyone to reform, so she'd resorted to finding fault with most everyone else.

The day after the party Kirsten had left Madison, vowing she would not come home until she was a famous actress. Over the next few years Ben and Peggy kept Abby informed about their daughter's apprenticeship. She progressed rapidly from walk-ons to larger parts. From the start she'd been kept busy with trade shows, summer stock, repertory theater, and even a few television commercials.

Finally she had landed the ingenue role in a revival of *Death Takes a Holiday*. She'd gotten excellent reviews and it seemed she was destined for stardom when she had suddenly married Nick Gabriel and had given up her career in order to spend more time with her husband.

Only five years later, Kirsten Bauman Gabriel was dead.

A shadow angled across the photograph and, starting guiltily, Abby looked up to find that Nick was standing over her. His face registered an immeasurable sadness when he saw what she was holding. He grabbed the picture away from her as if he expected her to offer resistance.

"I wasn't with Kirsten when she died," said Nick. "No one was. I was on a road trip with the Tigers and she'd stayed behind at our summer place in Detroit because she wasn't feeling well. I came home and found her . . ."

Leaving the rest of the sentence dangling, Nick carefully replaced the photo on the nightstand.

Abby felt compelled to say something, to sympathize. "She was incredibly lovely and so sweet," she said awkwardly. "I wish I'd had the chance to know her better. Her death was so tragic—"

"You're right about that, because she needn't have died. If I hadn't left her—"

"You didn't know what was going to happen! You shouldn't hold yourself responsible."

156

"Shouldn't I?" Nick stepped to the windows, opened the drapes, and stared out at the darkness. "The truth is that I am responsible. Kirsten's death was caused by a tubal pregnancy. It ruptured and she hemorrhaged. The pain must have been excruciating, but she was more frightened of doctors than she was of pain. She used to joke about it, say that if she ever broke her leg, I'd have to shoot her because she'd had enough of doctors and hospitals when she was a little girl."

Deeply touched by his flat recitation of the facts, Abby blinked back a rush of tears and cleared her throat. "Kirsten wouldn't want you to blame yourself," she reasoned.

"The hell she wouldn't!" Nick countered abrasively. "Kirsten didn't want to get pregnant in the first place, not with her pathological fear of doctors. I was the one who wanted kids, but I don't know whether she finally gave in or if her pregnancy was strictly an accident. I loved Kirsten, Abby, but I wasn't blind to her faults, and if you'd known her at all, you'd know how well she could nurse a grudge."

With a rueful shrug, Nick turned toward Abby and stood with his arms folded across his chest, leaning one shoulder against the window frame. His eyes were inscrutable as they roamed over her, reminding her that she was clad only in a sheet. For the first time she was terribly conscious of her nudity, and embarrassed by it.

"Since I didn't take any precautions tonight," Nick said coldly, "I suppose it's too much to hope for that you're on the pill or something."

"N-no, I'm not."

"Well, then, I trust you'll let me know if there's any—problem."

He'd spoken as if he was dismissing her! "N-Nick, I know something's wrong." By now she was so uncertain, she was stammering. "Won't you please tell me what it is. M-maybe I can help—"

"Nothing's wrong, damn it! But I think it would be a very good idea if you left now. I came back only to tell you that I've got an emergency on my hands. I have a number of calls to make tonight, but even if I didn't, I'm afraid I wouldn't be good company."

After a brief but telling glance at Kirsten's photograph, Nick's eyes locked with hers.

It was Abby who broke the eye contact. Unable to bear his remoteness and not knowing how to behave or where to look, she ducked her head so that her hair fell forward and veiled her face. She stared fixedly at her hands, which were clasped tightly in her lap, forcing back the tears that threatened to fall. She didn't look up even when Nick pushed away from the window and disappeared into the hallway.

She had no idea how long she remained huddled on the edge of the bed, shivering with shock at Nick's rejection. It might have been less than five minutes, or it might have been as long as an hour. It seemed like an eternity.

Awareness returned gradually. Her senses resumed functioning one by one, as if she were recovering from anesthesia. First she heard the wind rattling a shutter, then the rain tapping softly against the window, then the measured tick of the clock. Next her vision cleared and she saw the portrait of Nick's wife.

Haunted by the image of Kirsten's face, with its classic features, warm, liquid eyes, and hair like dark satin, Abby got into her clothes and walked back to the cottage.

Her mind remained mercifully numb until she was in her own bedroom. When the impact of Nick's treachery struck her, the force of the blow was so palpable that she ached from it. She felt empty and sick, but most of all she was assailed by an awful loneliness.

She fell into bed and pulled the covers tight under her chin and lay there stiffly, staring into the darkness until

158

her eyes burned. She was afraid to close them, afraid to fall asleep, afraid of what she might dream.

Just before dawn, her eyelids grew so heavy that she fled to the bathroom and took refuge under the shower. She scrubbed her body roughly, again and again, until her skin felt raw. But no amount of scrubbing could make her feel clean. She felt cheap and soiled and used. She had given Nick her trust and he had repaid her with betrayal. What for her had been an act of love had been nothing more than a few hours of sensual pleasure to him.

Anger took root slowly, but once the seed had germinated it grew rapidly, dispelling the terrible emptiness. It was rage that helped her survive the morning.

Jamie returned at lunchtime, happy as a lark and full of plans for the week's holiday. He ate a sandwich and changed his shoes at top speed, in a hurry to rejoin Shane and some of his other friends for a ballgame at Warner Park.

He tore his closet apart looking for his fielder's glove and finally located it buried behind his ice skates and hockey stick and the insulated overalls and sweater he'd worn on the February ski-club outing to Powderhorn.

As he was leaving the house, he stopped long enough to announce that on his way home he'd seen Nick.

"He was just pulling out of the drive as I was coming in," Jamie said. He fished around in the pockets of his sweatshirt, withdrew a baseball, and fingered it proudly. "Wait'll the guys see this!" he exclaimed gleefully, tossing the ball to Abby. "Check it out! It's autographed by the whole starting lineup of the Tigers!"

Abby caught the ball reflexively. She studied it without really seeing the signatures that were scrawled on it.

"Isn't that a terrific going-away present?" Jamie enthused.

"Going-away present?" Abby repeated blankly.

"Yeah. Nick had to leave town. He's been called away

159

on business or something." Jamie held out his hands, prompting Abby to throw the ball back to him. "Boy, oh, boy," he said, turning the ball between his hands and reading the names of his heroes as if he couldn't believe his good fortune. "Isn't Nick the greatest ever?"

CHAPTER ELEVEN

A week went by. After Sunday's rain the days were sunny and mild, but Abby derived no pleasure from the glorious weather. Usually she rejoiced in the springtime blossoming of the trees and the annual appearance of the daffodils and tulips and forsythia, but this year she was imprisoned in an icy cocoon of despair and her personal regeneration came by infinitesimal degrees.

On Tuesday it occurred to her that Nick had probably been secretly laughing at her adolescent confidences about sex. But while it was apparent he'd been bored when she'd foolishly babbled on and on as if the rapture they had shared was somehow unique, he had not heard her confess she loved him. That she had been spared this humiliation was a small comfort, but it was better than nothing.

She applied a heavier makeup than usual to cover the shadows beneath her eyes and reported to work at The Magic Lantern. She tried to appear unfazed when she found that an autographed picture of Nick had been added to the Fiores' collection and was prominently displayed so that she couldn't avoid seeing it when she sat at the piano.

Ginger and Tony inquired about Nick. So did Harlan

Crowley. When Harlan came into the lounge Wednesday evening, the first thing he said to Abby was, "Where's your young man tonight?"

Abby pinned an overly bright smile on her lips to mask the pain caused by this reminder that Nick hadn't even bothered to say good-bye, much less keep her informed of his whereabouts. Sidestepping the question, she replied, "He's not my young man."

"Well, you could have fooled me!" Harlan's faded blue eyes twinkled mischievously. "He looked at you as if he were starving and you were his own private banquet!"

Somehow Abby retained a semblance of control. Changing the subject, she asked, "Is there anything special you'd like me to play for you?"

Harlan was puzzled by her businesslike demeanor, but he was not offended by it. He took the hint and didn't pursue the subject until closing time. Then he made an oblique reference to Nick under the guise of reminiscing about his marriage.

"My wife and I were deeply in love, but we had our share of differences," he told Abby encouragingly. "That's something you have to expect with two strong-willed individuals. Lily and I celebrated our fortieth anniversary a month before she passed away, so I consider myself about as much of an expert on marriage as you're likely to come across, and I can tell you that love alone isn't enough to sustain a relationship. You have to keep working at it, but the more you put into it, the more rewarding it is. No matter how dark things seem sometimes, you've got to keep trying and you mustn't lose hope." He laughed his hearty laugh and could not resist jesting. "Just bear in mind that the first twenty years are the hardest."

Peggy telephoned on Thursday, requesting that Abby renew her promise not to go inside the main house.

"We should be home within a week or two," Peggy said,

162

"so don't worry about the plants. Nick tells me they're surviving nicely."

Although Abby was desperate to know why Nick had left so precipitously, she couldn't bring herself to ask Peggy what it was that had demanded his immediate attention.

Easter weekend came and went uneventfully, but on Monday an article in the newspaper explained Nick's sudden departure and shattered Abby's fragile composure.

After another restless night, she overslept that morning. She came into the kitchen just as Jamie was leaving for school. As he left the cottage to catch his bus, he called, "Hey, Sis, take a look at the sports section."

He had propped the paper next to her place at the breakfast table with the pages folded so that the relevant columns leaped out at her.

CY YOUNG WINNER TO STAND TRIAL

Chicago (AP)—Jury selection gets under way this morning in the courtroom of U.S. District Judge Otis Wirth in the trial of one-time pitching great Nicholas Gabriel.

At his arraignment last October, the former all-star pitcher was charged with felony violations of the Controlled Substances Act stemming from an incident of September 10. On that date, Gabriel and a former Detroit Tigers teammate, shortstop Leroy Collins, were returning from a series of personal appearances in Mexico when customs officials at O'Hare International Airport allegedly discovered two kilos of cocaine concealed in Gabriel's luggage.

At the time of Gabriel's arrest, his attorney, Richard Lorensen, maintained he would provide proof of his client's innocence and predicted the case would not come to trial. In a statement issued today, Lorensen says he remains confident Gabriel will be exonerated. If he is convicted, Gabriel faces a maximum sentence of fifteen years in prison and a $25,-000 fine.

Federal prosecutor Fred Kagan told reporters he expects the trial will last approximately one week.

Gabriel declined to comment on the charges against him. A four-time winner of the Cy Young Award whose blistering fastball rocketed the cellar-dwelling Tigers into contention for the American League pennant three consecutive seasons, Gabriel last gained national attention two years ago when injuries sustained in a motorcycle accident forced him to retire from baseball.

Abby read the article through twice before the fact sank in that it was not a colossal hoax. Gordon had told her about the criminal charges against Nick, and she had come to grips with the problem. She had witnessed Nick's reaction to her offhand remark about drugs, but she hadn't really thought that anyone could seriously entertain the notion that Nick actually might be guilty of such an offense. She was outraged that anyone could believe it, no matter how incriminating the evidence against him.

She turned the radio on and listened to it while she was going through her routine chores. She hoped one of the hourly news broadcasts would carry an update on the story, but there was none.

It was early afternoon before it struck her that through some horrible miscarriage of justice there was a remote possibility Nick might be convicted.

When Jamie arrived home from school, she discovered that he was also seething with indignation at the failure of the judicial system to recognize that Nick was incapable of such a crime.

"Did Nick ever mention anything to you about the charges against him?" asked Abby.

"Yeah, once. But I was the one who brought the subject up," Jamie reluctantly admitted.

"Well, what did he say about it?"

"Pretty much what his lawyer said—that he didn't think it was likely he'd have to stand trial."

"Did he say why?"

"No. He said—let me think." Jamie knitted his brows, trying to recall Nick's exact words. "He said something about it involving a confidence and that he wasn't at liberty to talk about it."

"And that's all?" Abby probed.

"That's all," Jamie slowly replied, "except that Nick wanted to know if you'd ever discussed his legal problems with me."

"What did you tell him?"

Jamie looked faintly surprised by her tenacious pursuit of the matter. "At first I told him I didn't think you knew anything about it because you hardly ever read the paper and you never look at the sports section. But Nick said he was sure you did, that Gordon would have told you about his arrest. So then I said you must not believe he was guilty any more than I did. I mean, you never objected to my seeing Nick or anything, and I knew you would have if you'd thought there was any chance he was into drugs." Her brother shook his head dejectedly. "I'm sorry, Abby, but that's about all I can remember."

"That's okay, Jamie." She patted his shoulder sympathetically. "I'm very glad you told Nick I don't think he's guilty."

"If he's innocent, the jury *can't* convict him, can they?" Jamie argued optimistically. "So there's nothing to worry about."

"Of course there isn't," Abby agreed, wishing she were as convinced of that as Jamie seemed to be.

When the six o'clock TV newscast provided what was essentially a rehash of the newspaper account of Nick's

165

trial, it required none of Jamie's urging to persuade Abby to place a call to Peggy. Hoping that the Baumans would have more information, they waited impatiently for Abby's call to go through.

As it turned out, though, Peggy knew only a little more than they did. When he'd heard the trial was to start, Ben had made an impromptu trip to Chicago to confer with Nick and give him moral support, but he hadn't contacted Peggy since his arrival, and she was as frustrated by the lack of news as Abby and Jamie.

"All I can tell you," Peggy said, "is that Nick never demonstrated any particular concern about the outcome until he phoned here a week ago. Then last Monday he sounded kind of down, but he told Ben his attorney still held out some hope that the trial wouldn't be necessary. Nick's been extremely mysterious about why Mr. Lorensen felt that way, so I really haven't a clue as to what sort of evidence they've been trying to turn up."

"Jamie and I would appreciate it if you'd let us know the minute you hear from Ben. We're very worried about Nick." Abby gripped the phone tightly to stop her fingers from shaking. "Or better yet, do you have a phone number where Nick can be reached?"

"I'm sorry, dear, but I don't. I don't even know where *Ben's* staying. He just hopped on the first plane he could get without stopping to make a hotel reservation. I'll try to get Nick's number for you, and if I can't, I'll be more than happy to keep you informed," Peggy promised in a gentle tone that told Abby her efforts to conceal the depth of her anxiety had not been successful.

The rest of that night and the following day passed with torturous slowness. In the agony of waiting for Peggy's call, Abby damned her impetuous behavior with Nick. If she hadn't succumbed to her desire for him, she would be free to go to Chicago and attend the trial. As it was, unless Peggy came up with Nick's phone number, she had condemned herself to making do with second-hand information.

In retrospect it seemed apparent to Abby that Nick felt he had been unfaithful to Kirsten's memory by making love to her. It was obvious that he deeply regretted his infidelity. When he'd looked at Kirsten's portrait that fateful Sunday night, the sorrow in his eyes had made his remorse painfully clear. In the light of this knowledge, Abby was certain her presence at the trial would be of no consolation to Nick.

As she had promised, Peggy telephoned on Tuesday, but the call only added to Abby's torment.

"Ben's a little worried," said Peggy. "As you can probably tell from the newspaper stories about the trial, the prosecution has a very strong case, and Nick's attorney seems to be out of his depth."

"How is Nick?" Abby asked tremulously.

"Not too well, I'm afraid. I haven't actually spoken to him, but according to Ben, he's adopted a fatalistic attitude toward the whole bizarre situation, and that's not at all like the Nick we know."

Oh, God, Abby silently lamented, *surely Nick didn't believe he'd done anything to warrant the punishment that would come with his conviction!*

At this thought she began to cry. All at once tears were coursing down her cheeks and, although she tried not to make a sound that would allow Peggy to guess she was weeping, Peggy must have known, because she added hastily, "Try not to worry too much, dear. Ben says Nick has come down with a nasty case of that flu that's been going around, so it could be that he's just not feeling up to snuff physically. You know how illness can sometimes affect a person's whole outlook. Besides, his friend, Leroy Collins, is due to arrive in Chicago tomorrow. Maybe he'll be able to cheer Nick up. Oh, and I have his lawyer's

167

telephone number. You can leave a message for Nick with him."

Abby tried the number Peggy gave her the minute they'd said good-bye. There was no answer.

She went in to work, but she kept on dialing the number at regular intervals until about eleven o'clock that night. When she still didn't get through to anyone, she did not try it again until early the following morning. Finally, at a little before nine o'clock, someone answered.

"Ogilvie, Baines, and Lorensen," said a crisp voice at the other end of the line."

"Is this the office of Mr. Richard Lorensen?" asked Abby.

"Yes, ma'am, it is."

"Well, I'm trying to reach a client of Mr. Lorensen's—Nick Gabriel. I was told I could leave a message at this number."

"That's right, ma'am. If you'll give me your name and where you can be reached, I'll see that Mr. Gabriel receives the message."

Abby gave the receptionist her name and telephone number. The woman assured her that the information would be relayed to Nick at the next recess and that he would probably return her call as soon as the day's proceedings were over.

Frail though they were, Abby clung to these assurances. But Nick didn't phone. It was the receptionist who returned Abby's call. The woman was apologetic but businesslike as she told Abby, "Mr. Gabriel asked me to convey his regrets that he is unable to talk to you personally. He said he was sure you'd understand, and he specifically instructed me to inquire if there is any problem he should know about. He said if there is—"

"No!" Abby cried.

"Ma'am?"

"Tell him no, there's no problem."

"Very well, ma'am. Is there any other message?"

"No—er, wait! Could you just tell Nick that Jamie and Abby are rooting for him?"

"Certainly, ma'am. Anything else?"

Yes, she had a message, her mind ran on. That she loved him with every fiber of her being, that she wanted more than anything to be with him now, to give him any comfort she could. A single word, Nick, she wanted to say, and I'll be with you. . . .

"No," Abby replied in a resigned little voice. "Nothing else."

After this Abby prayed that when Peggy phoned, she would have something encouraging to report, but when Wednesday's call came through, Peggy offered even less cause for hope than she had on Tuesday.

"I'm sorry, Abby, but tonight I haven't any good news to soften the bad," Peggy warned her at the outset of their conversation. "The defense is slated to present its opening statement tomorrow—probably in the early afternoon—and Rick Lorensen is threatening to resign because Nick's refusing to take the stand."

"Surely Mr. Lorensen must be bluffing," Abby protested heatedly. "He can't walk out on Nick now!"

"I don't know, dear," Peggy returned tearfully. "It looks almost hopeless. Ben told me that Nick won't listen to reason. He won't even talk to his brother."

"What about his friend—"

"Leroy Collins?" Peggy interrupted shrilly. "That's a laugh! It seems he's been subpoenaed by the prosecution and he's supposed to testify against Nick tomorrow. When they met today, he and Nick practically came to blows!" Peggy was crying openly now. "It's so unfair! Nick is innocent—I know he is—and after all he's been through the last few years, he deserves a little happiness. Instead it looks as if he may wind up with the dirty end of the stick all over again."

Now it was Abby's turn to reassure Peggy, but all she could think of were platitudes that weren't terribly applicable.

"Everything will come out all right in the end," she murmured. "It's always darkest before the dawn." As soon as the words were out, she winced at how Gordon-like she'd sounded.

If she had known how prophetic her remarks were, she might have slept that night instead of pacing the floor, but it was Thursday afternoon before Leroy Collins made his dramatic public confession.

"Evidently Nick's display of hostility and Rick Lorensen's bumbling were intended to demonstrate to Leroy how hopeless Nick's case was if he didn't tell the truth," Peggy reported exuberantly. "Leroy waited till things were right down to the wire, but he couldn't bring himself to lie on the witness stand. He broke down and admitted the drugs were his and that he'd put them in Nick's suitcase without Nick knowing anything about them."

Abby was light-headed with relief and lack of sleep. The living room swam in front of her eyes. Dizzy, she collapsed onto the floor and sat with her knees drawn up under her chin.

"Nick's been cleared?" she inquired faintly.

"Completely!" Peggy happily declared. "The judge dismissed the charges against him. He absolved Nick of any complicity and apologized to him!"

Abby laughed a little shakily, not quite able to believe that the nightmare of the past few days was over, and Peggy laughed with her. They chatted a little longer, and although neither of them made any sense, they understood each other perfectly.

Abby wanted to shout from the rooftops that Nick had been cleared. She did phone Ginger to tell her the good news. Jamie came home from school while Abby was still on the phone and when he realized what had happened he hugged her fiercely and let out a shout that was loud enough to be heard all over the neighborhood.

"Take tonight off and get to bed early," Ginger advised Abby when Jamie had settled down and Abby's ears had stopped ringing.

"Oh, Ginger," Abby demurred, still breathless from her brother's hug, "I can't take advantage of your good nature."

"Good nature, hell!" Ginger exclaimed lightly. "You look so miserable lately, I'm afraid you'll scare the customers. Seriously, Abby, I insist. I know you haven't been eating or sleeping like you should. Yesterday you looked as if you needed rocks in your pockets to keep a good wind from blowing you away. Please, if you won't do this for yourself, do it for me."

"All right, then," Abby agreed. "I will."

"Scout's honor?"

Giggling because there was no more improbable Girl Scout than Ginger Fiore, Abby pledged, "Scout's honor."

CHAPTER TWELVE

Abby was still keyed up when she went to bed that night, but because she hadn't had a full night's rest since she'd last seen Nick, she was also very tired. Exhaustion soon won out over elation and she had slept for more than two hours before something awakened her.

It seemed as if she'd just closed her eyes and her mind was fuzzy with sleep. She lay quietly at first, trying to determine what it was that had disturbed her. A storm had developed and it was raining fairly hard, but she didn't think it was the rain she'd heard.

She had nearly dozed off again when the sound of gravel rattling against the windowpane was repeated. Initially she thought this was part of the storm, but the third time she heard the noise, she was able to define the cause.

She climbed wearily out of bed and padded over to the window, opened the drapes, and looked out just as another handful of stones pelted the glass. Despite the darkness and the sheeting rain, she could see the tall, shadowy figure of a man. He was standing near the driveway, perhaps twenty yards away from the cottage, and he was looking directly at her window.

He bent over to scoop up another fistful of gravel from the drive, and the moment he moved she recognized the familiar lithe economy in the action. Her heart leaped to her throat as she pulled at the sash and opened the window.

"Nick? Is that you?"

"Yep," came the husky reply. "It's me." He moved a few steps closer, staring at her all the while.

"What in the name of heaven do you think you're doing?" she whispered irately.

"Returning your flower," he said, brandishing the white silk rose she'd worn the Sunday night they'd had dinner together.

"At this hour?"

"I got here as soon as I could," he responded in an aggrieved tone. His usually precise speech was slurred.

"Nick Gabriel, have you been drinking?"

"Nope, it's just this damned flu." He shook his head to underscore his denial and this threw him off balance, causing him to stagger nearer. "Don't be mad, Abby. Lemme in, sweetheart," he cajoled.

Now that he was closer, she saw that he was bareheaded and that he was not wearing a jacket or raincoat. The rain had plastered his shirt to his chest and was streaming down his face. He still swayed uncertainly on his feet. He looked so pathetic that Abby's irritation evaporated.

"Come around to the back door," she instructed him resignedly. "I'll meet you there."

Tossing a robe over her shoulders, she scurried out of her room and along the hall to the kitchen, turning on lights as she went. Despite his denial, she was not at all sure Nick wasn't drunk until she opened the door and saw that his face was flushed and his eyes were dull and opaque with fever. When he tried to step across the threshold, his legs almost gave way.

The flower fell unnoticed to the floor as he pitched heavily against her. Putting her arms around his waist, she fell back several steps before she was able to steady him.

"Lean on me," she offered unnecessarily. He had already hooked one long arm around her shoulders and was gratefully accepting her assistance. Before they had gone more than a few feet, she was panting with the effort of trying to support him. Since her room was closest, she steered him toward that.

"Haven't you any sense at all?" she scolded as she guided him toward the bed. "Standing out in the rain till you're soaking wet when you're burning up with fever!"

"Don't be mad, sweet Abby." He grinned crookedly down at her while she unbuttoned his shirt, pulled it free of the waistband of his slacks, and worked it away from his broad shoulders and off his arms. "I drove all the way up from Chicago just to see my girl. If I'm burning up, it's 'cause I needed to see you, but now that I'm here, I'll feel better in a minute."

The shirt dispensed with, he sprawled across the bed with his head on her pillow, using one arm across his forehead to shade his closed eyes. "Just need to rest awhile," he said, as if that explained everything.

"Nick!" Abby exclaimed nervously. "You can't fall asleep here!"

He opened one eye and glared at her. "Why the hell not?" he demanded. "I let you sleep in my bed!"

With a swiftness that belied his weakened physical condition, he seized her wrist, pulled her down beside him, and wrapped his arms around her. "Anyway," he said hoarsely, "I don't wanna sleep."

In the struggle of getting him to her room, she had lost her robe, and the heat that radiated from his naked chest seemed to burn through the gauzy fabric of her nightgown. She touched his forehead anxiously and, finding it scaldingly hot, tried to ease away from him.

"Nick, you're very ill," she reasoned when his hold on her tightened. "I'm going to call the doctor."

"Don't need a doctor." Turning so that he was lying half on top of her, he threw one leg over hers to pin her next to him and snuggled his head against her breasts. "All I need is you, Abby. Just you, sweetheart." Sighing deeply, Nick closed his eyes, and in the next instant he was asleep.

Now that Nick was no longer opposing her, Abby managed to squirm out from under him and roll him onto his back. Getting to her feet, she studied his recumbent figure worriedly.

Should she phone the doctor? She tested his forehead again and found his skin was even hotter now that the cooling rain had dried. Placing her hand on his chest, she felt his heart thudding against her palm. It was probably beating faster than was normal for him, but it was strong and steady. He was breathing easily enough too.

Recalling her own recent bout with the flu, she decided that if she could bring his temperature down, it should be safe enough to wait till morning to seek medical attention for him.

Hurrying to the kitchen, she filled a basin with cold water and added a few ice cubes for good measure. She armed herself with several hand towels and two thick bath towels with which to protect the bedding, and returned to her room.

Nick was resting just as she'd left him. Taking advantage of his unresisting state, she arranged the basin and towels and went into the bathroom to get some aspirin and the fever thermometer.

When she started to sponge Nick, he stirred and muttered protestingly at the icy sensation of the cloth on his forehead. While she wrung the excess water from another cloth, Abby bit her lip, praying that he wouldn't fight her.

His eyes flew open when she laid the towel across his chest. With an obvious effort, he brought her into focus.

"What the—"

"Shhh, Nick, it's all right," she murmured soothingly. "I'm only trying to bring your fever down a bit."

"It's cold," Nick muttered. His teeth chattered with the violence of the chills that shook him. "So damned cold."

"I know, darling. I know. But it'll be better soon."

His jaw clenched with the conscious exercise of will it required to lie still as she continued sponging him, constantly replacing the compresses with fresh ones, gently spreading them over his face and chest. His muscles twitched convulsively at the contact, but he didn't struggle, and she could soon tell that his temperature had started to drop.

He closed his eyes again and mumbled, "Did you hear about the trial?"

"Yes, I heard. Peggy called." She was relieved that his speech was less slurred. "Have you been taking anything for the flu?"

"Some medicine in the truck," he replied sleepily. "Damned stuff doesn't work, but I'll be fine now."

"I'm going to take your temperature," Abby said, and he opened his mouth cooperatively, allowing her to slide the thermometer under his tongue. While she waited for the thermometer to register his fever, she stood looking down at him, involuntarily admiring the powerful breadth of his chest and shoulders, the leanness of his belly and hips. She tried to force herself to look away, but she was impressed all over again by his rugged masculinity.

After the prescribed amount of time had passed, she removed the thermometer and he watched with half-opened eyes while she read it.

"Your fever is still a little over a hundred and two," she said. "I'd like you to take some aspirin."

176

Nick opened his eyes fully and she saw that they were clearer. "If you say so," he conceded grudgingly.

"I say so."

He braced himself on one elbow and she shook two of the tablets into his hand and offered him a tumbler of water.

Eyeing the aspirin crossly, he bargained, "I'll take them if you'll stay with me."

"I'll stay," she promised.

She smiled tenderly at him as he swallowed the aspirin and thirstily drank the water. In spite of his impressive size and the stubble of beard that darkened his jaw, he looked so very vulnerable with his hair all tousled and his lashes fanning onto his cheeks.

"Would you like more water?" she asked.

"Not right now." He lay back against the pillow and followed her with his eyes as she gathered up the towels and basin. "You'll come right back?" he asked anxiously when she carried them toward the hall.

Pausing in the doorway, she nodded. Although the width of the room separated them, the intensity of his gaze as his eyes roamed over her body reminded her of her scanty attire.

"I—I'll just put these things away," she stammered. "You'd better get under the covers now."

"Do you mean you're not going to help me undress?"

Abby turned away from him to hide the fact that she was blushing. "If you're feeling well enough to tease me," she retorted tartly, "you're certainly capable of undressing yourself."

He chuckled softly and she hastily left the room, pursued by the satisfied sound of his laughter. By the time she had locked the back door and turned off the lights, Nick was sleeping soundly.

She gathered up his slacks and shirt and draped them over the rack in the bathroom to dry. After dragging a

177

chair close to the bedside, she found the spare blanket in her closet and tried to make herself comfortable in the chair. Her muscles were achy and stiff from the strain of wrestling with Nick's considerable weight, and her eyes were gritty with fatigue. She knew she should be angry, but she wasn't. She felt strangely contented because Nick was here in her room, in her bed. She was ecstatic simply because he'd come back to her.

Savoring his presence, not knowing whether he might steal away with the passing of the night, she fought to stay awake and watch over him. But against her will her eyes closed and she lapsed into a fitful doze.

She woke several times during the night to check Nick's temperature. Toward dawn she discovered that he was perspiring lightly and she breathed a sigh of relief that his fever had broken. She had started to resume her cramped position in the chair when Nick's arm shot out to encircle her thighs and pull her down beside him.

"You must be feeling better," she gasped, surprised by his sudden attack.

"Much." He was holding her firmly and tucking the blankets around her. "I seem to remember you gave your word you'd stay with me."

"But I have! I've been in the chair all along."

"That's not quite what I had in mind." Burying his face in her hair, he groaned, "God, but you smell good—all soft and sweet and warm with sleep. This is cruel and unusual punishment! I want to kiss you so much it hurts, but I must be lousy with germs."

"Don't worry about it," she returned huskily. "I'm immune."

"Not to me, I hope."

Abby opened her mouth to reply, but she found it was impossible to speak. It was difficult even to breathe, for N   had impatiently pushed the straps of her nightgown
      houlders and he was crushing her painfully, won-

178

derfully close. With an inarticulate moan she melted against the hard length of his body and raised her lips to his.

He took her mouth with an almost primal urgency while his hands were kneading her breasts and molding her hips to his. With some magical homing instinct he was finding exquisitely sensitive spots and exploring the most secret recesses of her body, giving her intense pleasure.

His mouth left hers to trail hotly to her breasts and, at the gentle tug of his lips on the velvety roughness of a nipple, desire sang sweetly through her veins. She was bewitched by the riotous sensations of kissing and being kissed, of caressing and being caressed.

And when they were reunited, it was with a blaze of passion that consumed them utterly and left both of them spent and languorous with its fiery climax. Their hunger for one another appeased, they fell asleep almost instantly, still clinging together like weary children.

"Hey, Sis," Jamie called excitedly, knocking at the door to Abby's room. "Did you know that Nick's truck is parked in the driveway?"

At the rude awakening, Abby raised her head from its resting place on Nick's shoulder and stared at the door.

"Y-yes, Jamie, I know," she replied.

For a moment Jamie was silent. Then he said, "Oh! I see."

The three short syllables spoke volumes. They told Abby and Nick that Jamie *did* see, and the sound of his footsteps as he retreated down the hallway to the kitchen was exaggerated, telling them that Jamie was making as much noise as possible so they would know he had gone.

"I suppose I'd better go talk to him," Abby said. Her voice was tense with concern and her face was br͏ ͏ ͏th embarrassment.

Nick, on the other hand, was unconcerned. "Sweetheart, I'm sure Jamie is old enough to understand—"

"It's just that I've never done anything like this before!"

"Not true!" Nick chuckled. "You've done something like this *once* before."

When Abby reacted to his quip by tunneling under the blankets, Nick tried to peel the covers away from her head.

"Come on, sweetness," he coaxed. "Let me see your lovely face."

"No! Please, Nick, no! I just can't look at anyone just now."

For a moment he studied the slight mound she created, then he nodded thoughtfully. "If you promise me you'll stay here till I get back, I'll speak to Jamie."

"I promise," she said in a small voice. "Anyway, where else would I go?"

"Hold on to that thought, love," said Nick, patting the graceful curve of her derriere, "because if I have anything to say about it, from now on you're not going anywhere without me."

If Nick had waited for Abby's response, he might have seen the indignant stiffening of her outline beneath the blankets and been warned by it. But in a spurt of energy that was surprising, considering how ill he'd been only last night, he jumped out of bed. After some searching, he found his clothes in the bathroom. When he caught a glimpse of himself in the mirror, he grimaced at his disheveled appearance and rubbed the overnight growth of whiskers on his chin.

His shaving kit was still in the pickup along with the rest of his things, but he found Abby's razor in the medicine cabinet and used that. After he'd had a shower, he felt like a new man. He was whistling as he dressed and went off to square things with Jamie.

* * *

180

As soon as she heard Nick leave the bedroom, Abby threw the covers aside. She stalked into the bathroom and took a cold shower, but it did nothing to cool her temper. Her anger was unabated as she put on a jonquil yellow sundress that gave her confidence and made her look incongruously like a flower.

After she had combed her hair and applied lipstick and eye shadow, her fury would not allow her to sit still, so she made the bed and tidied the bathroom. This done, she waited impatiently for Nick's return.

She was eager to do battle. Her posture was rigid, her hands were clenched at her sides, and her eyes flashed an amber "caution" at him when he came back into the room. Without preliminaries she shouted, "You have the most gigantic nerve! You're the one who saw fit to take off without any explanation, yet you have the gall to imply that I'm the guilty party!"

Abby was so incensed that she didn't notice that Nick was grinning delightedly.

"Well, let me tell you, Nicholas Gabriel," she continued shrilly, "if you think I'll ever submit to your ordering me about—"

His grin finally registered, and she stopped in midsentence. Drawing herself up to her full height, she commanded regally, "At least be considerate enough to wipe that silly smirk off your face!"

"I can't help it, sweetheart," Nick countered smoothly. "It's just that now I *know* you love me."

Her glance was scathing. "I'm afraid I don't see the significance—"

"I'll bet you've never lost control and yelled at anyone else the way you've yelled at me," Nick said lightly.

Her anger wilted, leaving her weak and trembling with dread. "Oh, God," she whispered penitently, "I'm so sorry. Honestly I am. I shouldn't have—"

"Now you're the one who's being silly." Coming to her

181

side, Nick put his arms around her and held her comfortingly close. "I don't know where you got the cockamamie notion that you're not supposed to get angry at someone you love, but I'm a very demanding fellow and I want all of you, Abby. Not just your sweetness, but all your passions—and that includes your temper. When you're mad at me, I don't want you to whisper or play something belligerent on the piano. I want you to feel free to shriek at me whenever you think I deserve it."

"It looks as if I'll do precisely that whether you want me to or not," she admitted sheepishly.

Secure in his arms, she wrinkled her nose at him, which caused him to admonish her for her sassiness by kissing it, and then to kiss her mouth, and then to give her a practical lesson in how delicious it could be to make up after a quarrel.

Between kisses she asked, "Why did you leave without saying good-bye?"

"Because of the trial."

She pulled away from him and studied him gravely. "I find that hard to believe," she said. "Except for that day at the farm, you never seemed at all concerned about the charges against you. In fact, it bothered me that you were so carefree."

"You're right," Nick readily agreed. "I was carefree, but only in the literal sense. After Kirsten died, I stopped caring very much about anything. It was as if the worst possible thing had happened, and I'd lost what mattered most to me, so nothing made any difference anymore.

"Then I met you, and suddenly I cared—I cared terribly. But I thought everything would work out. Leroy Collins had signed a deposition that he was the one who'd been smuggling the drugs into the country, and Rick Lorensen was positive Leroy would back it up with a full confession in court. Then that Sunday night we were together, my brother Hank phoned and said Rick was trying to reach me, and when I called Rick he told me Leroy had gotten cold feet and was claiming he'd signed the deposition under duress."

"Oh, Nick, why didn't you tell me?"

"How could I?" With his hands on her shoulders, he drew her into his arms again. "How could I ask you to be part of my life when it looked as if I might be spending the next ten or fifteen years in prison?"

"But you didn't even say good-bye," she cried accusingly. "And you didn't return my phone call."

"I know, sweetheart, I know. I thought it would be doing you a kindness to be cruel. I tried to make you hate me so you wouldn't feel you owed me anything if I was convicted—not your love, or your loyalty, or anything else." Nick hugged her fiercely and pressed his face into her neck. "Treating you the way I did is one of the hardest things I've ever had to do," he said raggedly. "Can you forgive me for hurting you?"

"Yes, Nick," she cried softly, returning his embrace with artless abandon. "Oh, yes, darling."

Buffeted by emotions that were too deep to be expressed in words or even with kisses, for a few minutes they were content merely to hold each other.

This time it was Nick who moved away. "Aren't you going to ask what I told Jamie?" he prompted.

"Oh, Lord! I'd completely forgotten about him." Her expression was stricken. "How is he? What did he say?"

"He's fine. In fact by the time he left for school, he seemed to be delighted. We had a man-to-man talk about you. He told me that you're such a nut for cleanliness that if he gets up to go to the bathroom in the middle of the night, he finds you've sneaked in and made his bed before he gets back. But he loves you just the same."

Nick smiled at her confusion. "And I told him there was no need for him to defend your virtue because my intentions are strictly honorable. I also told him that he'd better get used to seeing a lot of me because you and I are going to be married as soon as we can get the license."

"Married! B-but we hardly know one another!"

"That's very funny," Nick exclaimed dryly. "I'd have said you know quite a lot of important things about me, but if you want a résumé, I'm thirty-five, in sound health, reasonably bright, and in possession of all my faculties. I'm financially independent, so it'll be no problem for me to support a wife and family. My teeth are my own, and I don't drink to excess, gamble, carouse, or chew. I love kids and dogs, but most of all, I love *you*. Is there anything else you want to know?"

When Abby didn't respond, Nick tried to appear crestfallen. "Don't you want to make an honest man of me?"

"Please be serious," Abby pleaded. "Marriage isn't a joking matter."

"Do you love me?" he persisted.

"You know I do!"

"Do you doubt that we're compatible?"

Her eyes shied away from his. "N-not really."

"I love you, Abby," Nick declared solemnly. "I want you to be my wife."

Still refusing to meet his eyes, she inquired tremulously, "What about Kirsten?"

"What about her?" Nick cupped Abby's face between his hands and made her look at him. "I loved Kirsten, Abby, I won't deny that. And I won't deny that we were happy together, mostly because neither of us demanded very much of the other. If we had—well, the point is, we didn't. We were like a couple of kids playing at life, but that was another time and another me. I've paid my dues since then and I'm not a child any longer. Now I want my reward, and you're my reward, Abby. It's you I love, and it's you I'm asking to share the rest of my life."

Abby was crying openly now, but her face was luminous with happiness, for Nick was looking at her as if she were

184

infinitely precious and absolutely essential to him. He was looking at her as if she were his whole world, and she knew their love was made in heaven and touched by magic.

"Do those tears mean you'll marry me?" Nick began kissing them away.

Smiling radiantly at him through the tears, she nodded. "How could I ever forgive myself if I passed up an ex-ballplayer who still has all his teeth and doesn't chew tobacco? You must be the only one of your kind!"

Nick chuckled appreciatively and nipped at her ear in sweet retaliation. "Since I'm such a rarity," he whispered, "don't you think it's high time you showed me how much you love me?"

"Yes, Nick," she conceded wholeheartedly. "Oh, yes!"

And willingly, joyfully, wantonly, she did.

LOOK FOR NEXT MONTH'S
CANDLELIGHT ECSTASY ROMANCES™

When You Want A Little More Than Romance—

Try A Candlelight Ecstasy!

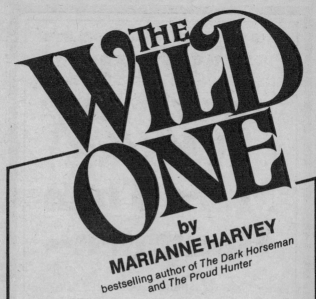

THE WILD ONE

by
MARIANNE HARVEY
bestselling author of *The Dark Horseman*
and *The Proud Hunter*

Proud, beautiful Judith—raised by her stern
grandmother on the savage Cornish coast—
boldly abandoned herself to one man and sought
solace in the arms of another. But only one man
could tame her, could match her fiery spirit,
could fulfill the passionate promise of rapturous,
timeless love.

A Dell Book $2.95   (19207-2)

Once you've tasted joy and passion, do you dare dream of

LOVING

Danielle Steel

bestselling author of
The Promise and *To Love Again*

Bettina Daniels lived in a gilded world—pampered, adored, adoring. She had youth, beauty and a glamorous life that circled the globe—everything her father's love, fame and money could buy. Suddenly, Justin Daniels was gone. Bettina stood alone before a mountain of debts and a world of strangers—men who promised her many things, who tempted her with words of love. But Bettina had to live her own life, seize her own dreams and take her own chances. But could she pay the bittersweet price?

A Dell Book ============================== $3.50 **(14684-4)**

The second volume in the spectacular Heiress series

The Cornish Heiress

by Roberta Gellis

bestselling author of
The English Heiress

Meg Devoran—by night the flame-haired smuggler, Red Meg.
Hunted and lusted after by many, she was loved by one man
alone...

Philip St. Eyre—his hunger for adventure led him on a
desperate mission into the heart of Napoleon's France.

From midnight trysts in secret smugglers' caves to wild
abandon in enemy lands, they pursued their entwined destinies
to the end—seizing ecstasy, unforgettable adventure—and
love.

A Dell Book   **$3.50**   **(11515-9)**